My real name's Kez. I
disappeared.

And Silver Wind's disappearance is just the start of all the trouble for Kez. She is taken away to be fostered, miles from all her Traveller friends, and it seems that no one is even looking for her mum. Then she meets up with Stefan and Joe, whose efforts to help are blocked at every turn. It appears that someone, someone high up, is trying to stop Kez finding her mother. But why would anyone kidnap a Traveller? And how is the bad-tempered farmer whose land they were camped on involved in all this? Trying to find the answers leads Kez, Stefan, and Joe into terrible danger.

Patrick Cave was born in Bath, Somerset, and educated at Wells Cathedral School, St Martin's College (Lancaster), and the University of North Wales. He has taught English in various parts of Britain and Greece, and currently lives in France, having moved to work at Bordeaux University. He believes that children's fiction is the purest and most honest form of telling the stories of our existence. 'It's a pity,' he says, 'that when we grow up we often learn to paint life pictures with very drab and limited horizons and then find that we have to live there ourselves.' When he is not writing he enjoys cross-country running, tennis and skiing, as well as music and 'green causes'. *Number 99* is his first novel.

Number 99

Also by Patrick Cave

Last Chance

Number 99

Patrick Cave

OXFORD
UNIVERSITY PRESS

OXFORD
UNIVERSITY PRESS

Great Clarendon Street, Oxford OX2 6DP

Oxford University Press is a department of the University of Oxford.
It furthers the University's objective of excellence in research, scholarship,
and education by publishing worldwide in

Oxford New York
Auckland Bangkok Buenos Aires
Cape Town Chennai Dar es Salaam Delhi Hong Kong Istanbul
Karachi Kolkata Kuala Lumpur Madrid Melbourne Mexico City Mumbai
Nairobi São Paulo Shanghai Taipei Tokyo Toronto

Oxford is a registered trade mark of Oxford University Press
in the UK and in certain other countries

First published 2001
First published in this edition 2002

British Library Cataloguing in Publication Data available

ISBN 0 19 275271 5

1 3 5 7 9 10 8 6 4 2

Typeset by AFS Image Setters Ltd, Glasgow

Printed in Great Britain by
Cox & Wyman Ltd, Reading, Berkshire

1

My real name's Kez. I only became Number 99 when Mum disappeared.

It's pretty strange writing this, talking to someone I don't know. It was Troll's idea to write it all down. A sort of story or something. He said if I did it right people would enjoy it like with an adventure book or a thriller, but also that they need to know the kind of things that are going on under their noses in this sparkling, half-tamed island. (This 'comfortable democracy' was what *he* said.)

Anyway, if I'm not much of a writer now, maybe I'll be better by the end. Sorry, I'm smiling saying that, 'cause the end is a long way off and I could be down at the edge of the woods with Joe. Listening while he tries to learn the guitar Troll gave him.

You better know from the start that I'm a Traveller. I live in an old Bedford bus with Mum. Troll's got an ambulance and there are other vans too. Sometimes as many as ten, though the police are better when we don't have too many. I can feel myself getting angry now (silly!!!) because I know that most of you will already think 'crusty' or maybe 'poor girl, it's no kind of life for her, is it?'

I've heard people say this so often. People stuck behind net curtains with huge TV sets. Uggghhh! Listen, it's every kind of life for me. Our bus is warm, bright, lovely, but I live in the world, not in a box. I have a nose stud and dreads, but no that doesn't mean I'm not clean. I don't care what other Travellers do: *we* look after our sites, and people work when they can. Well, I do care really. You wouldn't want me to think of *you* like I thought of some thief or idiot who just lived in another house in your street, would you?

I want you to realize that I like my life and I probably know just as much as you do, only maybe about different things, because I'm not always in school.

I'm laughing now 'cause Troll's just read what I've put over my shoulder and he said:

'Hey, is this going to be an adventure story or a manifesto for an alternative and caring lifestyle?'

That's how he talks by the way. He can't help it.

OK, well this thing started almost exactly a year ago. I was thirteen then and we'd found a really lovely place to live for a while, somewhere in Hampshire, I think. A little bit of rough grass with a few trees at the edge and some big rocks dotted around, all sandwiched in between the corners of some huge wheat fields. Our spot was a bit higher than the rest—the fields sort-of curled up at the corner—so we could look right across the wheat for miles, a spiky pale olive-green carpet that you could almost see and hear ripening in the heat.

(There. Just like a real writer. Cross-eyed face!)

I don't know why the weather was so scorching—it was only late spring—but it was a good chance to sort out

2

all our gear, get the washing done, work on the vans. We never waste the good weather when it comes. Of course I love the winters too, freezing mornings when you put on everything you own to go and get wood and *still* feel icy. That kind of thing makes me smile 'cause you know you're alive whatever else. And once the stove's lit the bus will be like toast all through the day and deep into the dreamy-sharp winter night.

That one morning when everything stood on its head was beautiful, despite the rest: the orange-pink of the first sun caught in the mist and . . . BUT I only saw *that* when I'd managed to grab something to put on: the first thing was lots of noise and three policemen almost ripping the door off its hinges and stamping in like we were an IRA safehouse or something. I HATE that. We leave the door unlocked, but that's not so those idiots can act out their stormtrooper fantasies. The bus is our home, our space.

Mum wasn't there and I guessed she'd slipped out to walk or watch the sun come up or mess about with plants (she'd taken her specimen bag too). The three gorillas seemed a bit peed off to find just one girl inside, but of course it doesn't matter how old or who you are if you're a Traveller: you can't be trusted! So they got a policewoman in to watch me dress in case I crawled out through a back window or started trying to destroy evidence.

Huh!

Outside our little site had turned ugly with blue uniforms. All the rest of my mates (about fifteen) had been shoved out like me shivering and swearing . . . or taking the peaceful, rising-above-it-all approach and happily checking out that bronze-age dawn. None of it was new: the idea is that the hippies get to watch their homes being searched and then gone over for safety, paperwork, and all that. ('Did you know your left-hand wiper is missing its rubber, *sir*?' . . . 'Yes, officer, that's why we don't drive in the rain' . . .) Between the sense of invasion, legal hassles with the vans, convictions for bits of grass, and the damage that gets done ('accidentally') we're supposed to see that it's easier to give up our mad, awkward lives and settle down normally like good lambs.

In case you think it all sounds like a good idea, just sit quietly a moment and imagine (really imagine!) it happening in your home, police breaking in through the door maybe three or five times a year, going through your private stuff, making you feel like dirt.

Of course that's different, though. Being a Traveller is illegal. They made a law for that in the eighties under Thatcher—who Troll calls 'you-know-who' with a ghoulish laugh.

If Mum's not there for any reason Troll usually fields me because I can get really upset and sometimes just can't help biting back. Once, when I was ten and saw all my stuff getting thrown out the bus window I picked up our heavy splitting axe and threw it through the windscreen of a police car. I *think* I'm learning the rising-above-it thing but Troll and Mum keep me close when we get turned over.

Everything went pretty much as usual this time, except there was one nasty moment when a really beautiful couple who sometimes travel with us—Jake and Krissy (pregnant and also my soul-sister; we often work together doing batiks and stuff for festivals)—got told they were going to have their van towed away.

Jake lost it for a bit. That's what the police hope for.

The rest of us, not kicked out of our homes *this* time, were supposed to be packed up and moved on by midday and the force were going to stay and make sure. Well fine, I was used to it, so I got the bus up together and turned the engine over to make sure no last-minute mechanics were needed. The police didn't like *that*, a little girl firing up a bus!

4

Then . . . no Mum.

It's funny. People always think that 'no kind of life' thing I said before, as if you were some neglected little flower needing looking after, BUT they also at the same time think that a Traveller girl of thirteen should be hard as nails, not able to have normal feelings.

When midday came and my mum still wasn't there I was upset. In a state, in fact, because that wasn't like her. But the smooth-faced, grinning monkeys from the force thought I was putting it on or covering for her while she did something iffy . . . i.e. burglary or something. *Covering for her!!* Those idiots couldn't see how I felt; didn't see it as I was watching all my mates' vans crawling away down the lane to head west (to some other squad's patch, where we would meet up again) and didn't see it even when they radioed for a truck to come and get our bus and told me to sit in the police car to get taken to their station.

The WPC said, 'You sure you got a mum, love?'

I didn't even answer. Her trying to jolly me along, I guess, or I might have hit her.

Troll had stayed to keep me company and said he was coming too, in the panda.

'And you are, sir?' They put that *sir* bit on the end to take the you-know-what. Also, they must have already known his name from the van checks.

'Callum Potter.'

'And what is your interest here, Mr Potter?'

'Kez's mum and I are close. We're all family really.'

I could see that Troll was not far off getting his stutter, which he does sometimes when there's pressure like that, but he looked the sergeant in the eye and was very cool and polite and when they said, 'You can follow in your own . . . vehicle . . . Mr Potter,' he said no, he was coming with me in the police car.

Troll is a hero.

The sergeant decided it was easier to give in in the end and then had to radio for someone else to get the ambulance. The Goddess knows why they always do that, tow the vans away instead of driving them. Are they worried about being seen by their mates in something that has great spreading purple flowers painted on the side, Glastonbury Tor on the back, and *small economics help us survive* on the sunstrip?

'Probably about £2000 in taxes to get us moved on today,' Troll whispered in the car, but by then I was crying a bit and looking out the window. A good thing I hadn't done a tarot for today or I might have given up altogether. At that point I still thought that Mum going missing and the curse coming on was as bad as it was going to get.

Then it was the station bit.

'Your mother's name?' Another sergeant, tired, unbelieving, and yellow-grey, like a nicotine stain. Why do people *do* what they do with their lives?

'Silver Wind.'

We looked at each other while he considered.

'Is that her first or surname?'

'Well, all of it really.'

It was like I'd handed the sergeant a blue banana or a giant fish, still wriggling. His pen hovered over different bits of a form. Then he decided to try a smile (gruesome!) and what he probably thought was a nice uncle-like voice.

'But she must have another name, young miss: come on now, *you* know, a real one, like . . . (for a moment the poor guy couldn't think of a single ordinary name and next to me Troll was shaking) well, like Bev Allsworthy or something.'

He'd turned pretty quickly from yellow to red and miserable and I thought it just had to be his wife. He couldn't think of any name for a woman except his wife's name. He thought it was only real if you were with someone called Bev Allsworthy who made you unhappy and glad to get to form-filling at work. He should have found a Silver Wind.

Sometimes I get so sad.

I told him seriously and clearly: 'My mother used to be called Dr Rachel Harrison. She's thirty-three. She often goes out walking, but not for so long. She has long dark hair and green eyes and she's thin and happy.'

He filled out his form with relief and phoned 'upstairs' to get them to check Mum out on the computer or something. Troll and I sat on hard chairs and drank warm machine-tasting tea, not knowing what giving that name was going to bring.

Afterwards, I couldn't believe how easily we got separated. The desk sergeant's phone went again and he listened and looked at us and nodded and said, 'Yes, sir, right, sir, I understand', then he came over our side of the counter and asked Troll to speak with him privately a moment in an interview room. Clever that, leaving me sitting in the lobby like I was going to be there all safe and in-view and making Troll think they were treating him like my guardian or something.

'Back in a mo, Kezzie,' he said cheerfully and I didn't see him properly again, my rock with his roots going right down into the living earth, till maybe two months later.

By the way, this isn't a story about the police or how corrupt they are or anything like that. The raids and the harassment really do happen and you've got to know what it's like from my side if you want to know me. But I've met some really great policemen and I see now that it's as easy for me to think of them all as one identical group (silly) as it is for them to do the same with me and *my* lot.

Silver Wind always says to me: 'It's the negatives that go with time, as your spirit sees more clearly. The fears, guilt, regrets, suspicion of others.'

Pretty deep stuff and I know most of you will think she's off with the fairies and probably me too . . . but, well . . . your negatives will go with time. Giggle.

Anyway it was only about thirty seconds after Troll left the lobby that another door from inside the main part of the station opened and a WPC, very friendly looking, a bit untidy, with freckles and not wearing her hat or uniform top, put her head round the door and said, 'Kez Harrison, is it? Just going to make some coffee and sandwiches for you and your friend. You must be starving! Why not come through and give me a hand? Help to pass the time. Your friend can come through too when he's ready.'

It was lovely not to be looked at and feel like some sort of specimen and I *did* want something to do because in my mind I'd started imagining rape and murder and all the worst things. With the girl being friendly I could feel more tears coming and in fact I did get pretty weepy over the sandwiches but she was cool and bright and let me get on with it without making a fuss.

Then someone knocked on the little room where we were and another woman came in. I could see right then that *she* was the gushing, mothering, snobby, sour sort, with so many barriers up you've got no idea what she really is inside.

'I'm Mrs Cotterell, dear,' she gushed: 'Brenda if you like. I'm what they call a social worker—do you know what that is, dear?—and I'd like to have a little word with you. In here, why not?' She said it like she'd just thought of it, that moment.

Behind Mrs Cotterell, *Brenda*, came the sergeant from the raid and before I knew it he'd got rid of the WPC and the sandwiches ('I'll leave them with your friend, then, for when you're done.') and it was just the three of us. Him leaning against the wall and just staring at the other wall, while I got to sit opposite Brenda. She got out some files and papers. I thought that her eyes were too small over her permanent smile and wafting scent.

'Now, dear,' she said, with all those papers spread out in front of her, 'let's start, shall we?'

I was soon hating the WPC for fooling me.

And myself for not being quite as switched-on as I'd thought.

2

'As the officers haven't managed to contact your poor mother yet, I think we're going to have to find somewhere for you to stay. Just for a day or two . . . until she turns up, dear. Don't worry, it'll be with a *very* nice lady, who often has children in her house for a little while when they need it. Like you, you see?'

Bang!

How did we get *here*?!

Forty minutes of boring questions, friendly-sounding with lots of 'dear's and wafts of chemically perfume mixed with the sergeant's mints, while Brenda went poking about in my life. Yes, my mum was a real doctor, not medical but a botanist and horticulturist, and yes she really was called Silver Wind, she'd filled out the forms and all that. No, I had no father living with us, but Troll often looked after me and did lessons and stuff if I wasn't near a school. *NO* he did not touch me! Not like she meant.

I tried very hard, the hardest I could with those small, busy eyes on me, to make her see.

'We're just normal. Like anybody. Except that we help each other, the whole lot of us. I eat proper food and sleep in a bed and learn things and I'm almost never ill and no I do not have sex with anyone. I'm thirteen.'

The eyes slid unfocused over me and she waffled on, not wanting to know. Maybe I'd been wandering a bit till I heard her say that about a place to stay.

Wake up, Kez!

When I realized what she wanted to do, I was very very close to totally losing it with the old trout, even if it just got me locked up to calm down. There was only *one* problem, which was Mum being missing, and she seemed to be blind to that. I started thinking in panic that nobody was even trying very hard to find Silver Wind. And then I wondered—quite suddenly and clearly like a cold plunge— if for some reason getting *me* packed off somewhere was really what it was all about. All the hurtful poking about in my life trying to find things wrong was just an excuse.

Why hadn't I even been asked what Mum might be wearing, where she might have walked and all that? Wasn't that normal if someone disappeared? I opened my mouth to ask . . . and then shut it again. Think. Wake up! If they weren't trying to find Mum now, there wasn't much point telling them anything new . . .

But then maybe Troll had told them everything they needed to know in some other room?

'You wanted to say something, dear?'

Brenda's face was greasy with make-up in that stuffy room: too large across the table. It made me feel sick.

'Yes. I need a tampon.'

'I'm sorry, dear, what?'

'A tampon. Tam-pon. Or I'm going to bleed on the chair.'

The raid sergeant, dozing against the wall, looked disgusted. Maybe they thought Travellers didn't have periods. Anyway, he went scurrying off and came back quickly and gingerly gave me one, not meeting my eye. (Hard man gets squeamish at menstruation!) And that gave me the chance to spend some time in the loo, cooling off, wondering what to do.

The one thing I really wanted to do wasn't possible as there were bars over the tiny loo window.

I finished in the cubicle and then stood on the washbasin and looked out anyway. Next best thing was to walk straight on down the corridor and try and get past the front desk. If only I could see Troll again, I thought he could sort it all out for me. Where on earth *was* he?

A moment later I knew where he was. In the car park, right across the other side, getting into a panda car. I watched in a dream the car start and reverse out of the space and leave. Then my legs just went under me and I half jumped, half fell off the basin and barged back into the loo to throw up. I could feel prickles of sweat on my forehead and back and I was pretty dizzy, light-headed.

Troll wouldn't leave without me.

When I couldn't throw up any more, I cleaned myself up at the basin and looked in the mirror. I was white and pinched and looked like death. Just like the scruffy, no-good hippy-crusty girl Brenda wanted me to be, needing to be sent to a nice lady to get the corners rubbed off and taste proper food.

Troll wouldn't leave unless he thought I'd be waiting for him at the ambulance or maybe with the others.

For another queasy moment when I almost had to be sick again I thought maybe they'd found a body or something and he'd had to go and say if it was Mum. Maybe they were just keeping me out the way to protect me.

No, that was wrong. Even across the width of the police tarmac he'd looked cheerful and glad to be getting away from the place. Troll was nuts about Mum: there couldn't have been bad news. And Brenda and the sergeant certainly weren't trying to *protect* me. I was washed out and worried and hadn't eaten since yesterday and they were planning to stick me with some 'nice lady'. Now they'd somehow got my only friend to leave.

Finally I felt myself calming down, the panic went, and a little piece of ice in me decided that Brenda and that lot could get stuffed. Since they were so sure I was the hardened, rough, crusty girl, that's what I would give them. (And PLEASE, I added to whatever spirit might be listening, let Mum be OK.)

You know, writing that last bit and remembering, about me being in the loo, got me so wound up (like not being able to breathe for a moment) that I had to stop and put on some music and tidy up a bit. I wish you could see our bus. We've got loads of batiks and Nepalese embroideries and stuff hanging over some of the windows and dividing off our 'rooms' and sometimes they need to be taken out and given a good shake and spread out to air. Then I found some spring flowers at the edge of the wood and lit some incense and did the washing up. So now I'm renewed ('The therapy of entropic work,' Troll would call it!) and the bus is too. I wonder if you think I'm nutty or if you understand.

Leaving the loo, I walked right on down the corridor to the security door that went back to the front desk. No code or buzzer or anything needed from the inside. One or two uniforms and lots of glances (amused or suspicious) but nobody saying stop. Even the desk sergeant let me go on past.

I couldn't resist saying, 'Goodbye, Sergeant Allsworthy' just to see if I was right about his name and I was still grinning at the way he started lifting his hand to say goodbye when I got outside and found Brenda puffing on a fag and speaking into her mobile.

' . . . well, too bad . . . yes . . . it's the only place if she's got to go today, so whatever *he* thinks we'll just have to . . . '

And then she saw me and dropped the phone, the bright plastic bouncing off down the steps. What *really* surprised me was how angry she seemed in that moment, way over the top for me just coming outside, even if she guessed I was going to head off.

She didn't say, 'Hello, dear, where are you off to then?': she just plain grabbed at me.

Well, Brenda on her own would have been OK—she was down on her fat arse by the time reinforcements arrived, her face dark red, and saying stuff that I'm sure social workers aren't supposed to say to little disadvantaged girls needing protection—but I only made it halfway to the car park entrance before I was brought down myself.

All change. That was it as far as the caring image went. From then on I wasn't left alone for a moment and back in the sandwich room Brenda hardly bothered to speak to me while she made her arrangements and filled out her papers. I was pretty sure she was writing any old rubbish just to get it all done the way she wanted, and I was also sure that she knew I knew that. Just occasionally she glanced up and saw me watching her and she was almost smirking like some kid at having got her way.

Oh yeah, that sickly frozen smile from before still hung around. Was there now a whiff of something harder and colder behind it? Just then, with the pains inside doing their stuff in waves, I was too shaky to know or give a stoat one way or the other.

The afternoon went on and I sat on my orange plastic chair and was given tea but no food, so I spooned in lots of sugar (which I normally don't have) to get some energy back in case I got another chance to run. It didn't seem possible that it was still the same day. In my mind I could see Silver Wind moving quietly through the wheat stalks in the pre-dawn, brushing the swelling heads with her fingertips. She always touches plants like it helps her to understand them better. I sent up a big prayer to the great Goddess of all fertile things to keep her safe and didn't even know I was crying again until someone said to me:

'Kez. We have to go. Sorry.'

It was the WPC again. The one with the sandwiches. Next to her Brenda was standing clutching car keys and her big shiny bag and looking impatient.

In the car park the tarmac was still warm but the sunlight was starting to turn orange so maybe I'd dozed on the chair. A big dark green car, not a police car, was just in front of the steps and we all got in; the WPC with me in the back, Brenda up front, driving.

The police station where I'd been turned out to be in Basingstoke, and I thought I'd just be taken somewhere else in the town—somewhere I could scoot off from quickly unless they wanted to watch me twenty-four hours a day—but instead Brenda got us on to a fast arterial and then a motorway, leaving Basingstoke behind us in a golden haze it didn't deserve, and I started taking much more notice of what was happening so I could try to get back soon and catch up with my friends to do a proper search for Mum. It was lucky I'd put on some decent kit when they pushed me out of the bus in the morning as it looked like I would be having to sleep rough for a couple of days walking back.

Every time an exit came up on the motorway I willed Brenda to take it, but the car went on down the fast lane and the orange behind us changed to red and then died completely, while strings of lights blossomed in lines heading into the dark east.

When it got too dark the WPC looked up from the book she was reading and said, 'You do realize this is a seventy limit, Mrs Cotterell?' and Brenda sent her an irritated look over her shoulder and slowed down to a bit less than eighty.

The WPC frowned.

'Where ARE we going?' I asked to anyone that wanted to answer. 'I thought I was being taken to a "nice lady" for a day or two? Until Mum gets back. Not stoating China.'

I thought Brenda was going to just ignore me but she snapped back, 'Not China. Camberwell. Which is in London.' And I could hear that smirk in her voice again.

Beside me the WPC's frown got bigger (and I doubt I looked exactly happy . . . London!!!), but after a moment she gave a little shrug and said to me, 'It's a Mrs Payne. Rose, I think. She's supposed to be really nice. Loads of experience doing this; looking after children, I mean.'

She sounded apologetic and gave me a quick, bright smile which I couldn't help returning. It made me think that she wasn't on Brenda's side after all.

I said, 'OK, so big deal, she's nice. You know, I had lots of nice, kind people to look after me this morning. Now my mum's disappeared and nobody seems to be doing anything, and the guy who's sort-of-a-dad was tricked into going away and all the rest of my mates have been sent off too. What's happening? Why do you lot want to stick me in London? Why not back with the other vehicles? Or at least in Basingstoke, close for when Mum turns up?'

The whole thing was so idiotic I thought my questions hardly managed to break the surface and I just ended up saying again: 'What's happening?' Even to me it sounded like a little kid's question, sort of desperate and vague.

The WPC looked at me with real sympathy and said, 'Mrs Cotterell?'

Our driver was quiet for a minute and then glanced back again, though now it was too dark to see if it was the same irritated look. Just a dark lumpy shape against the bright little lights on the dashboard.

'She's only got *herself* to blame for not being told more. If she'd managed to be a bit more *civilized* . . . '

She trailed off, maybe sensing that the WPC wouldn't think much of her for saying that in front of me—wasn't a social worker supposed to protect and understand kids?—but there was still some muttering from the front and I heard the words 'savage' and 'discipline' floating back. Big deal. I'd heard at least as bad and usually much worse from strangers in the street and honestly didn't mind what Brenda felt: she couldn't loathe me any more than I did her!

Then she twisted round (hairy at that speed!) and said, 'All right then, young lady. I suppose you have a right to know. We're taking you to Mrs Payne, who is what we call a foster parent, for a little while because we do not view your companions on the road as suitable guardians. Mr Potter, for example, has no blood ties, no children of his own, and a criminal record. No doubt the Basingstoke police will bring me in again when your mother turns up and we can all have a . . . rethink, but in the meantime we needed a place for you to stay and there was nothing in Basingstoke at such short notice. As I usually work in South London and happened to know Mrs Payne was not fostering at present, it seemed best to take you there. The *authorities* mercifully agreed with my assessment. Satisfied?'

Troll's record was for possessing two grams of cannabis and chaining himself to a cruise missile transporter, back in the eighties. He'd taught me to write and sing and do quadratic equations and about Thomas Mallory rotting in jail while he wrote about King Arthur and about the big guns pounding at each other across the mud and bodies in the First World War. Also, I could strip an engine down and put it back together.

Outside, the great glowing jumble of buildings that was London replaced the blackness. I thought of the carpet of wheat and ached for its smell and sound. Big cities were always a bit of a nightmare for me. The Goddess was given no space here to lift up her children.

The big green car stopped-and-started its way deeper and deeper into the horrible mess.

The WPC said, 'If you want to let your friends know that you're OK and all that, I might be able to give them a message. The one we're holding anyway, you know: from this morning.'

I must have looked pretty blank, as she said, 'You know, Kez, the one with the baby coming. I think he'll probably get let off with a caution and allowed to go in the morning as he didn't actually hurt anyone. Can't promise, of course!'

Jake. They had Jake! And I didn't even know when I was in the station. I thought he'd been allowed to go off with the others.

The rest of the journey I was writing something for the WPC—Barbara, she said she was called—to give to Jake when she got back. I did it on the back of an old envelope (all she could give me) leaning on her book.

It felt so good to have some way to talk to someone I knew—someone on my side—that the last half an hour went quite fast. But when I handed Barbara the bit of paper there was such a strong feeling of anger coming from the front seat, sort of a silence that you could hear, that I wondered if Brenda would try to stop Jake getting my message. Could she do that? It didn't seem likely that social workers could tell the police what to do . . . but then that sergeant from the raid had let her carry on any old how.

If I wasn't totally wrong about her, imagining it all or something, then *why* was Brenda so angry? Why did she want me in London so much, out of touch with my friends?

There was something I was missing here.

3

Ooooaaahhhhh.

Groan.

Yawn.

The bed seemed to want to swallow me. Great lumps
and folds of mattress pulled at my limbs and squishy clouds
of duvet, leaking feathers, made getting up like swimming.

Outside, a never-ending thundering, vibrating rumble
said, 'Welcome to Camberwell.' Wherever *that* was. Not
anywhere I planned to be for long.

Mind you, standing in my grubby underwear in front of
the clouded wardrobe mirror I thought that the first thing
was to get a bit cleaner, in case I had to hitch or something.
And to eat! I felt like I hadn't had a thing for a week, but
somehow last night I'd been able to stay awake long enough
to eat eggs, tomatoes, fried bread, some sort of pea soup,
and a great stodgy slice of cakey pudding, with Mrs Payne
smiling and nodding, saying, 'That's it, dear. Another one
of these, why not? Or some toast now perhaps?'

The pudding was like the mattress.

Everything in Mrs Payne's house seemed worn and lumpy if it was material, like the armchairs, or dark and gloomy if it was wooden, like the wardrobe in my room, which took almost all of one wall. But it was all clean and somehow the feeling of the house managed to be like Mrs Payne herself—positive and sensible.

I'd known at once that she was OK. It's easy to tell if people have a problem with my appearance (the hair and stud!) or my lifestyle and all that, or if they think I might be human.

'Lovely to see you,' she'd said, like I was her favourite niece visiting. 'I've got the kettle on and I expect you could do with some hot food.' Her way seemed to be to act like we already knew each other, which was actually great after being a hooligan and a criminal for the rest of the day. Also, she made certain that Brenda was in and out as quickly as possible and I was pretty sure they didn't like each other at all.

'You've got such a long drive back, poor dears,' she'd said, waving away the papers Brenda was fumbling out of the shiny bag. 'Oh, send anything on later if I *must* have it, Mrs Cotterell. Kez and I are just going to have a nice meal and then bed. All that paperwork must drive you barmy.' And she rolled her eyes at me while Brenda crossly re-fumbled her files back into the bag so I felt that it was Brenda out of all of us who was alone and unwelcome.

Somehow that helped a lot when the green car drove off, back to where Silver Wind was still missing and where Troll was probably still looking for her (or for me?), leaving me in this strange place.

I suddenly thought that maybe what I've written hasn't told you properly how frightened I was. Like I said, lots of people think a hard Traveller girl doesn't feel frightened or sad or anything like that. We're supposed to have a dog on a bit of string and just be worrying about change for the next can of Special Brew and be easy to get into bed, if you can bear the smell.

Well, of *course* I was frightened. Not mostly for myself, 'cause I knew I could catch the others up, with time . . . but for Mum. My beautiful, graceful, gentle Silver Wind who gave me my life and who trusts too much sometimes, though she thinks it's the other way round.

I almost couldn't cope with the fear about Mum, but I knew I had to be patient and face my own situation first or I wouldn't be any help to her if she needed help, and also I knew that whatever the police did or said, Troll would be looking for her. The message I'd given to Barbara for Jake said not to come after me but to concentrate on her. I'd be there soon to help, one way or another. Nobody would be able to stop me.

When I went downstairs Mrs Payne had breakfast spread out ready—'You go on, Kez. I've had mine, dear.'—and carried on with the acting-like-we-knew-each-other thing.

'A bit of shopping this morning, do you think? I'm sure you could do with a few bits and bobs.'

She didn't ever in all the time we spent together ask me any questions about me or Mum or the life I usually had, unless it was something I started talking about first. Not much seemed to bother her (Brenda???)—she stayed zappy and practical—and I found out why while we were sitting on a red number 12 bus grinding up to the funnily-named Elephant and Castle for our 'bit of shopping'.

'Do you know what?' she said to me. 'You're my Number 99.'

'Umm . . . sorry?' I didn't have a clue what she meant.

'Number 99, Kez. There have been ninety-eight other children staying with me before you. I'm already in the *Guinness Book of Records*, you know.'

I sat and boggled at that bit of news for a while. Maybe that was why the bed was like it was, I thought. It explained anyway why she didn't get hassled easily!

'And this afternoon, dear,' she added, 'you can meet Number 1. He's coming to tea.'

I guess I should tell you what Mrs Payne—Rose—looks like, although I'm not very good at that and often don't remember after meeting someone anything about their appearance. I keep a picture of people in my head, but it's not what they look like, more what they feel like. I'm not trying to be difficult or different or hippy-ish or anything: it's just what I do. (If I met somebody famous in the street, Tony Blair or someone, I'd only recognize him because I've seen him move and smile or give some things from inside freely while he hides others: not because I know how far apart his eyes are or his hair colour.)

Going round the horrible indoor shopping centre at 'the Elephant' I saw the two of us in some mirror glass and was really surprised to find that Rose was fat. Somehow she seemed thin and brisk and sharp (in a nice way) but in the mirror she was fat and quite slow in a maroon mac, with dark curly hair mostly gone grey and a kind of heavy face. Maybe you've seen a sailing boat or something covered with an old tarpaulin so that it's all shapeless and lumpy and faded, but when you whip the tarp off there are lovely clear lines and shiny varnish and you can see that the thing was made for cutting through the water and dancing about on the waves. Well, Rose is like that in my mind.

She is a rose.

Together in that glass we looked a pretty strange pair and I felt self-conscious and defiant at the same time about how I looked, which was normal when I was in a town. Even if you feel good inside, it's impossible (for me anyway—smile) not to get wound up about what the crowds of people round you think. Of course, some of them usually look barking to me too . . . *and* uncomfortable in some of the awful stuff they wear, suits or chunky hundred-quid trainers or the Goddess-knows-what! The Elephant shopping centre wasn't too posh, though, and I don't think anyone paid us much notice, except perhaps in the shops in case I was going to walk off with something.

The 'bits and bobs' turned in the end into quite a lot of kit and, seeing Rose parting with her cash, I said, 'I'll be going back to Mum soon, maybe even today . . . just some underwear maybe . . . '

But *she* said, 'It's all right. Brenda Cotterell's lot will pay for all this, so don't worry, dear. Why not think of it as a present from Mrs Cotterell?' which made me laugh. Also, she didn't try to make me buy what *she* thought was the right thing: she let me choose and just said things like 'Why not get seven pairs, Kez, for the whole week?' or 'Would some jeans be useful?' To be honest, I'd never really been shopping like this for so much kit at once, and I found myself enjoying it . . . a lot! Doesn't take long to get hooked.

We finished by checking out some market stalls that were set up outside. I was going through some rails of second-hand clothes when I saw the van parked up behind that stall was plastered in old festival stickers . . . Glastonbury, Trowbridge, The Elephant Fayre (More elephants . . . but I promise this isn't secretly a story about elephants, either!), Larma Tree and others.

The *cool* thing about how I look and living the way I live is that with the right people I know I'll be accepted and able to be myself. I smiled at the girl doing the stall—spiky blonde hair, mauve jeans and top, and slightly faraway eyes—and said 'All right?', and she smiled back and said 'All right? Having a chilled day? Great rays! Wish I could pack this lot up and get out to somewhere a bit greener.'

'Me too,' I said. I glanced back to Rose, who was looking at sunglasses on the next stall, and made up my mind. 'Hey, I'm looking for a lift down towards Basingstoke or maybe a bit further. Got separated from my people after we got moved on yesterday and the *soash* have stuck me up here for some reason.' (The 'soash' is the social services, by the way). 'The others'll be waiting for me.'

'Oh, babe, that's rough! Been there, done that myself! But we don't head down that way for another week . . . plenty of space then if that's any good.'

A week! No, I would already be back with Troll and Mum by then, I was sure. I thanked her and said I'd get something together myself.

'No problem. Anyway, I'm here every morning till we go, so if you change your mind . . . If there's some bearded lunatic like a pirate doing the stall instead of me don't worry, he's mine and he doesn't bite. I'll tell him you might show up.'

Rose drifted on back and said, 'Found anything nice, dear?' and actually I *had* found something while I was talking to the mauve girl. A black velvety jacket with tails at the back. Not like anything I usually got but I loved it. Good old Rose didn't bat an eyelid at my strange choice and asked how much.

'Lovely, isn't it?' said the girl. 'Would have had it myself except it was too small.' She came out from behind the stall and helped me try it on, standing back to look. 'Cool! I think you were meant to have it, babe. Love it when fate does that, don't you?'

So she gave me the jacket and a hug and told me to take care, and Rose said, going back on the bus, 'I've been shopping south of the Thames for forty years and never been given a bean, let alone a hug! I think you must have something special, Kez, to be liked so easily.'

I didn't explain it was just because I was a 'crusty'!

OK, I know I said I was planning to get off back down to Basingstoke as soon as I could, but I *didn't* go that day and didn't even know that the chance would be gone tomorrow.

I thought that with the message to Jake, who'd be out of the cells and seeing Troll today, that they'd know where I was by now and would probably get the number from Barbara and phone me or something. But obviously they would be concentrating on Mum . . . and to be really honest, looking back now I think I was frightened by what they might find and so was sort of distancing myself to get used to the idea of . . . whatever. Of course another part of me was completely desperate to be there!

Tell me what you'd have done?

And one other thing. I realized that I already had some sort of . . . connection with Rose. I'd have to tell her if I went, but then as my foster parent she'd probably have to tell someone else and I'd be rounded up again and put somewhere worse. Not telling her, just going, seemed impossible. I wouldn't have minded with Brenda, but I thought Rose deserved, well, respect or something.

Sometimes life gets incredibly tangled up, doesn't it, but you've just got to try and do the right thing. Otherwise it all comes back on you anyway and you're worse off than before.

Well, by the time Number 1 arrived at Rose's place that first afternoon I'd put leaving off till tomorrow and then, like I said, it was too late. He, Number 1 that is, put all the rest out of my head for a while by drawing up outside the little terraced house in an E-type Jaguar. He must have been late thirties or maybe more and was dressed in a suit. Not really what I'd expected from one of my foster brothers! Although most things about how he looked—hair colour and height and all that— were pretty average as far as I could tell, I thought he probably had lots of girlfriends, because he was one of those people that can make you feel like you've got all his attention and deserve it. *Sickeningly* polite, interested, happy to make an effort for you and not a guy who sees a problem without charging in to try and sort it for you.

But deep too, I realized after a bit. The openness was just manners to him, I think, or maybe a defence wall.

'Number 1, meet Number 99,' Rose said, with a bit of a giggle. 'Stefan, this is Kez.'

Stefan reached out a hand to shake mine and said, very seriously, 'Delighted and charmed to meet you, Number 99. Rose has told me almost nothing about you, but with your consent perhaps we could put that right over tea?'

Then he beamed a huge smile directly at me like a missile and I'm embarrassed to say that even though I was sure he was taking the piss, I blushed and couldn't get a word out to say back to him!

Cringe! Even now.

Even more silly, and making me really angry with myself, all through the tea I felt as if I had two heads or had just crawled in from the gutter . . . not because Stefan made me feel out of place, but because he *didn't* (if that makes any sense). Unlike Rose, he asked me directly both about my normal life and what had happened to put me here.

'Leave the poor thing alone,' Rose said, but he replied, 'I think that one waif and stray has the right to ask another about her circumstances.' And put like that, thinking of him on the lumpy mattress, I had to agree. In fact, it was a lot easier to relax a bit when I remembered that we were both in the same sort of club. Numbers 1 and 99. Except that I was just playing at it, of course, and would be back with Mum and my mates soon.

I think he knew what was on my mind—getting back to Basingstoke—as I told him about the day before, and he also must have guessed some of the fears I had, because when I'd finished he said, 'How would it be if I gave the police station in Basingstoke a call, Kez? Just to see what's going on.'

I wouldn't have thought of that, but he made it seem so easy . . . just picking up the phone and asking the operator for the number and then speaking to someone where I'd been yesterday, all in his very polite and posh-sounding voice. It was like me with the girl in mauve, knowing the rules or something, only Stefan and I were also now in the same club and so perhaps knew some of the same rules, I thought.

Rose sat fatly in her chair with chubby hands in her lap, the sharp lines hidden under the tarpaulin, and let him get on with phoning. Somehow she'd managed to deal with ninety-seven others, apart from the two she had there in her front room. Some of them must have been desperate, hurt from where they'd been, beaten up maybe. Maybe even Stefan had been. *Her* club was the biggest of the lot, I thought, and not nearly so easy to see as my dreads or Stefan's suit.

'I see. Well, thank you for your time.'

Stefan rang off, looking puzzled.

'Well, Kez, I'm afraid you'd better brace yourself. I don't understand it, but the officer to whom I spoke said that there may have been "some hippy" (his words), name unknown, in the cells, but that he'd been transferred last night and he couldn't tell me where. Furthermore, he said that there was no ongoing search for your mother, as they had been unable to turn up any records of a Silver Wind ever existing and so had come to the conclusion that you'd been "spinning them a bit of a yarn" (his words again) to avoid being taken into care.'

He stopped and I couldn't think of what to say. Rose's gloomy, old-fashioned clock ticked away on the mantelpiece, while the three of us sat in silence. I was scared and confused and I wanted to go to Basingstoke and break all the windows in their stoating police station and then start on the cars. Like I had with the axe before, but all the way.

Mum!

After a minute I said, 'Troll? The others?'

But Stefan gently shook his head. 'I'm sorry, Kez. The damned fellow said he didn't have any other information. Started asking me who *I* was and what was my connection with this business. Ordinarily I would have pulled rank on him, but . . . something made me decide just to end that particular conversation, for now anyway. I wonder . . . '

He sat and stared into space for a minute, like he was concentrating on something, and then re-focused on the room and said cheerfully:

'How about a run down to Basingstoke tomorrow, Kez, for a look around? That's if *you* don't mind, Aged P?'

'I don't mind, if you keep my girl out of mischief,' was Rose's reply.

Mine was more difficult to get out. I wanted to jump on him and kiss him to bits for suggesting it, but if I did that I might end up weepy again, so all I could do was nod like an idiot.

I managed to get some control back as he was leaving.

'Beautiful car,' I said, 'but it's missing on and off on one cylinder. Never worked on a Jag, but I might be able to sort it out for you.'

Stefan's turn not to know what to say.

Justice done.

4

There were loads of things I wanted to ask Rose about Number 1, but she wouldn't answer most of them. Said I'd have to ask him myself about anything to do with his past and how he'd come to her. One waif and stray to another. (That was one of the rules of this club maybe.) All I really learnt was that she'd had a husband then and they'd decided to do that, fostering, because they couldn't have kids. And Stefan had been with them much longer than any of the others . . . for ten years.

'But what about now? What did he mean about "pulling rank" with the police? He's not one himself, is he?'

'Lord love us dear, no! My boy's far too bright for that. He's some sort of civil servant is all I know, because he likes to be mysterious . . . *but* I think he's quite high up whatever it is.' She sounded proud and I guessed that he really was her Number 1.

In the morning Brenda's paperwork came with the post. Great wodges of it.

Rose said, 'We'll have to sit down and try and do this lot together later—when you get back—as there'll be lots of things I need to ask you.' She sighed. 'I hate forms, don't you?'

I didn't have much experience of forms, but I was sure that if I was given the chance I could also learn to hate them. Smile.

'You know, it's a funny thing, but usually the local office—Brenda Cotterell's lot—check on me daily with a new charge. It's all supposed to be very carefully monitored, you see, to make sure you're settling in all right, not thinking of running away or anything. (Did she give me a tiny questioning look?) Someone visits or telephones most days at first, and there's always a lot of what they call *ongoing assessments* and all that to do. They know it drives me half potty and so they cut it down as much as they can and try not to bother me . . . after more than thirty years of fostering, you see? . . . but *some* of it has to be done by law. Well anyway, as nobody got in touch yesterday I telephoned them myself . . .'

She stopped and I suddenly thought that she wasn't sure about telling me whatever it was after all. That made it pretty easy to guess what was coming.

'And they hadn't heard of me?'

Her kind, troubled face gave me the answer.

'Like the stoating police!' I was furious, really wound up and frightened with whatever it was that was happening.

Rose touched me for the first time since my arrival, came and put her arm around me and gave me a squeeze.

'You shouldn't worry, Kez, not really. I'm sure it's all just the . . . bureaucracy and that. They did say that our Mrs Cotterell might not have transferred all the files up from Basingstoke yet or something—idiot woman—and that they'd try to get hold of her. It's probably all nothing.'

I thought she believed that about as much as I did. But it was nice to have the hug—we hug and touch a lot usually at home (in the bus!)—and my anger went down a bit. I still had an hour till Number 1 was coming so I went upstairs and did some yoga and breathing in front of the gloomy wardrobe and then washed and put on some of the new stuff. A deep fire-red skirt and the new black jacket from the stall. Had to be glammy for the E-type and the suits. The choice of shoes was either new trainers from yesterday or my normal boots, so I went with the boots in case we ended up going through the wheat or something.

When Stefan roared up the street—in jeans and roll-neck—he teased me about looking 'refined', which made me almost bite his head off, as I felt self-conscious enough anyway.

'It's just so I don't embarrass you, with your car and suit and your posh voice! Because you're doing something nice for me. I'm very happy being what I am, thank you!'

He looked a bit put out for a moment. Then he said, 'I was only worried, dear fiery 99, that you wouldn't want to work on my old car in all your finery. You did promise: I'm relying on you.' And so that was cool and we laughed.

It was easy to believe that he was 'something high up' in the civil service. He seemed to find it pretty simple to pull *my* strings.

One thing about me, something that'll make you think I'm totally cuckoo, if you don't already, is that I don't like being too comfortable. Not just physically, I mean, although that too, and there's no way I could spend my life in some double-glazed, semi-detached, insulated nightmare . . . but also in my spirit. (Phew: rant avoided, hey?) I like being at peace sometimes, with the yoga and music and spending time alone, but challenges and risks and even pains are good too, sort of keeping you in touch with your limits. And all that stuff—love and the cold and not knowing when you're going to die and everything that comes with being alive—keeps you hungry for the little miracles.

So maybe in spite of being without Mum and worrying and feeling the police and the soash and everyone was against me . . . maybe part of me was also really alive, thrilled by what was happening.

Not maybe. Definitely.

When we set off I found that being in a bright yellow E-type was no different in the end to being in a bus covered with purple flowers. Everyone stopped to look at you. They don't get quite as long to look with the E-type, true, except in places like Camberwell Green, with the long rounded nose of the car inching its way across between lines of red buses and other traffic. Sitting so near the ground we were right in the scummy bottom of the thick pollution porridge and could have done with some sort of breathing tube sticking up above the lot.

London's got a real vibe of its own. Buzzing energy and pretty exciting sometimes. But then your car suddenly breaks free of the heaving traffic and groaning mish-mash of buildings and your heart slows down to normal and your skin remembers what fresh air feels like. Lots and lots of fresh air if you're in an E-type with the windows right down.

Stefan didn't like motorways, so we went on normal roads. With the wind and engine noise and Stefan's stereo we spent most of the journey not speaking. Speaking would have been shouting. I didn't mind that: I'm not much good at what 'adults' call *small-talk*. Of course Troll and most of the others are 'adult' really, but we don't do that stuff about the weather and football and how one thing you can buy is better than another thing. And I didn't really feel I knew Stefan well enough to ask him what I was really interested in . . . about being a waif and stray.

' . . . !' Stefan had his head turned to me and was saying something.

'WHAT?' I screamed.

'I SAID . . . ' he screamed back, 'WHAT ABOUT THE POLICE STATION FIRST, JUST TO MAKE SURE, AND THEN A DRIVE AROUND NEAR WHERE YOU WERE STAYING?'

'COOL,' I yelled.

We parked opposite the police station instead of in the car park and spent a couple of minutes deciding if I should go in with him or not. *I* wanted to go right in and see the look in their eyes if they tried to lie to me. I like to tackle stuff head on. They could hardly say I didn't exist if I was standing there in front of them! *And* I wanted our bus back, or at least to get some stuff from inside for now. If they said there was no Silver Wind, then the stoating thing must be mine according to their logic. But Mum's certificates for being a doctor and her name and everything were inside the Bedford too, and if I could get those they'd look pretty silly trying to say I'd 'spun them some yarn' about her.

Stefan wasn't quite so sure.

'I see how you must feel, 99, but I really believe we should play our cards a little closer to our chest than that, to begin with at least. Just supposing . . . it's not likely, I know, but just supposing there *is* someone in the police or the social services who is deliberately lying to us, perhaps because they bear you or your mother or friends some kind of ill will . . . well, we don't know who that person or persons is-stroke-are, we don't know why, and most of all we don't know what kind of clout they've got. If it was just an ordinary constable or the man on the desk or something that'd be one thing, but the man I spoke to yesterday claimed to be CID . . . and then there was that conversation Rose had with Camberwell Social Services. Brenda Cotterell will certainly have had to get her fostering papers signed by several figures in authority, even if it was only supposed to be a temporary thing . . . ' He trailed off for a moment. 'Listen, Kez, let's just walk softly shall we and let *them* do any guessing?'

Softly softly. Not my strength.

So I gave him any names and stuff I could remember and we decided between us how he would handle it and then after he'd crossed the road and disappeared into the building, to stop myself going nuts waiting (and maybe going in there after all!) I cranked up the bonnet of his car and started checking the HT leads and plugs to see why that cylinder sometimes missed.

It *was* one of the leads, but I started the engine to make sure and then of course I realized that I was a total, stoating no-hoper. A uniform was coming along the pavement, not one from the raid or anything but just an ordinary PC, finishing his beat maybe.

'Good morning,' he said cheerfully. 'Off for a joyride are we? Or is the car yours perhaps? If the latter, perhaps I could see your licence, young lady.'

They must spend their time at police school learning to speak like that. So unnatural and sarcastic.

'Oh *yes*, I just take this when the Roller's being polished.' I couldn't help being sarcastic back, but they hate that of course and this one stopped smiling and got a lot more businesslike at once.

'Right. Would you please close the bonnet and I think we'll lock the vehicle and just go and talk about your Roller across the road there.' i.e. the station! The station where Stefan was even now supposed to be playing his cards close to his chest. He might not be too impressed if I was hauled kicking and screaming in there for trying to steal his car, I thought.

Well, I could just run off and lose myself, but then the PC would almost certainly report the 'attempted theft', along with my description and probably a check on the car . . . or I could tell the truth that the car's owner was in the station now and get taken over there for confirmation and probably get recognized and asked why I wasn't in Camberwell. Hmmm, those two ideas didn't seem much like the low profile Stefan wanted, so I went for Plan C instead . . . lying.

'The owner is my uncle, officer. He's a rock star, though he hates getting recognized. He's just down at the shops in the centre, but he parks up here so people don't see the car . . . I can get him to look in when he gets back to tell you it's all OK if you want.'

Plod was not looking impressed.

'I do love a good yarn. Just a minute, though, it's not Elvis is it, your uncle? My missus'd be over the moon if I got Elvis's autograph!'

We shut up the car (he turned off the ignition and kept the keys) and I was taken back over the road and through the car park where I'd last seen Troll. Oh gods and goddesses, the last thing I needed was to be shut up in that crummy station again, making sandwiches I didn't get to eat, and waiting for whatever they decided should happen to me. Right now, Rose and Camberwell seemed really quite nice.

With the hard grey steps where Brenda had tried to collar me just ahead I decided to try Plan A after all and run for it. At least there was some chance then that Stefan and I wouldn't be seen together and his plan of playing it cool would stay possible, as long as they didn't catch up with me, of course! Anyway, I just wasn't going to get stuck in there again answering silly questions.

Plod's hand was just lightly on my elbow because he thought I was 'coming quietly', as they say—and also they have to watch how they touch female prisoners these days—so I took a couple of long slow breaths as we walked, counting four in, four holding, four out, and then dropped quickly down and forward, like I'd just tripped, so he had to let go. The next bit was to sprint across the car park and hope for better luck than last time I did that. But just as I set off and Plod launched himself after me with the cliché, 'Oi, come 'ere you!', another voice shouted 'Hey!' and I stopped short, the policeman almost knocking me down as he barged into the back of me.

Stefan was standing at the top of the steps, half laughing I think because he'd only been gone for a bit and I'd already blown it so badly, and half serious for the same reason.

'Uncle Chas!' I said, 'Fancy you being in *there*! This policeman thinks I was trying to steal your car.'

I could feel the waters rising. Soon we would all be back inside and I doubted the tea would have got any better in two days.

'Oh yes?' he said weakly. 'And just what was it that *you* were doing to make the officer think that?' I could hear the *you daft idiot* on the end even though he didn't say it. Luckily, though, he didn't question the name change or the 'uncle' bit and I thought we *might* just be OK, with his posh accent and everything.

And then Plod said, 'Obviously a misunderstanding, sir, and apologies for that. I wonder if you have any ready documents for the car you could just bring inside a moment so we can clear it all up properly?'

The message in Stefan's bemused eyes finally penetrated my skull: *What will I say when my paperwork doesn't say 'Chas Someone-or-other'? What, Kez, is my story supposed to be?*

All he said out loud was: 'Ah, yes of course. There *might* be something in the car if you'd care to just come back over the road for a moment.'

He was able to push Plod's buttons as easily as he had mine and we all started moving away from that bad-news doorway again; but I knew it was up to me to help with the next bit. So I said, as chattily as I could, 'Of course, Chas is only his stage name.'

'Chas? Chas what?'

'You're kidding! You really don't recognize him? If you had a teenage daughter she'd be in tears right now, just seeing him! My mates never stop giving me grief to come and meet him.'

All right. I know. Cringe.

We were at the car now and while Stefan rooted around in door pockets for the right stuff he took his cue and made noises about it being better if it wasn't known he came shopping here and better to use his real name with the police, in case of bad publicity.

'The tabloids positively hound a man, don't they, officer?' he said chummily, as if the PC would know anything about being hounded by newspapers.

Poor old Plod was left racking his brains for pop stars called Chas something and we got into the yellow car and left, crisis averted.

Stefan turned to me as he drove and said, 'Chas the pop star! And at my age? You really are a clot, Kez. I felt more like half a comedy double act!'—Which I didn't think was very fair. No, OK, you're right: it *was* fair. Goddess, it makes me squirm just thinking about it.

'Fixed your car anyway,' I said, sulkily. 'What did *you* find out inside?'

'I'll tell you,' he said, driving into a pub car park, 'over lunch. And, Number 99 . . . cards close to our chest in here, OK? No comedy setpieces?'

We went inside and ordered some very unsuspicious cheese rolls.

'So?'

Old cheddar and pickles spilt out of a roll that seemed to have got rigor-stoating-mortis.

'So . . . not brilliant I'm afraid . . . ' He stopped and looked at me with that very direct look and I thought he was wondering how tough I was and whether I was up to hearing the truth.

I must've passed.

'Worse than the telephone call, in fact. I asked for Sergeant Allsworthy and they said he was on leave, and the same thing for WPC Barbara-something. Then a CID man appeared, a Sergeant Gregg, and wanted to know who I was and why I wanted Allsworthy. I think he might have been your raid sergeant . . . tall, square shoulders, getting a bit of a belly, dark-going-grey and a moustache already gone that way?'

I nodded. 'I think so, yes.' (Like I said before, I'm not good with faces. What *I* could remember about the raid sergeant was a kind of clumsy, confused strength . . . inside as well as out. A snuffling boar, I'd thought.)

'Well, I'd say that whatever's going on, he's one that we shouldn't trust. The other people, out the front, had been very civil and friendly, however unhelpful. But Sergeant Gregg believes in more of the bullying approach. When I told him that it was a personal matter, he started reading the riot act about wasting police time and hindering officers from carrying out their duties. I got the distinct feeling that he wanted to threaten me, perhaps make me give more away, but that he couldn't because I wasn't a known quantity . . . and for all he knew I might have been quite harmless.'

'So no chance to ask about Mum? Or Jake?'

'I think it would have been pointless, Kez. Perhaps very foolish. Much better for them to assume you're just tucked up in Camberwell in your new foster home waiting for *them* to contact *you*, like a good girl. So far, after all, anybody who could help us or tell us something has been . . . well, removed from immediate view, shall we say.'

I stared bitterly out of the window. It was another roasting day, especially in the velvet. I was almost looking forward to seeing my wheat sea again and how far it'd ripened in the last two days, but the place would be empty now. Stefan was kind, bringing me down here, but let's face it, we weren't exactly finding out a lot, apart from the Basingstoke police and probably social services here or in London or both being dodgy. I really needed to find some of my own kind, someone I could relate to. I wanted to *do* something, not just trail around in a flash car while Stefan's posh voice got me accepted in country pubs but didn't get Silver Wind back, or Troll, or my home.

Maybe I could steal the bus back from the police compound! Or at least get off west, hitching, to try and catch up with whoever was left from our last site. They wouldn't have gone far, not if they were worried about Silver Wind or me.

I realized Stefan was watching my face and he said, like he'd been reading my thoughts, 'There is another way, 99. I know you must be itching to act, but really, trust me, it would be better to be patient for now. Give me a day or two and I might be able to find something out.'

It didn't feel like he was stringing me along. I thought he must have something definite in mind.

'Rose Payne said you were something high up and

mysterious in the Civil Service.' To be honest I didn't really know what the Civil Service was. Not people *I* ever met, which probably suited both of us.

'Rose is . . . proud of me, I suppose, and she likes to exaggerate a little. I just have a very ordinary job, mostly at a desk covered in dull papers.' He paused and glanced down at his plate and then said casually, 'It *is* true that I could at least make a few small enquiries to colleagues who . . . owe me a favour or two. It's not much, but it might be worth trying.'

Trust me, he'd said, but now he said it wasn't much, his idea. Well, would *you* have believed that? With that pause and everything? He was on to something, and looking at his face right then, very calm on top but definitely fizzing away deep underneath, I thought that he was worth trusting.

'OK. I won't bolt off for a few days.'

Promising that was almost physical pain, and also relief.

'Great! So, coffee first, and then a drive around looking for clues, my dear Watson?'

The barman was leering at me. The same guy that hadn't wanted to let me in to start with.

'Can we forget the coffee?' I said.

When I was standing on our site again, an empty space where we had sung and worked and lived for a while, I surprised myself by crying. You must think I cry a lot by now, and I suppose it's true. But not usually because of fear or pain or loss, or not those things without their opposites too at the same time, if that makes any sense.

Where we are now is beautiful, every bit as good as that other place surrounded by the wheat, perhaps even better. This spring has been more normal (the weather, I mean!)

and the woods near here are filled with flowers, the trees are heavy and moist. If you walk right through those woods, the land drops down and you come out near a small river. That's where Joe goes for his secret guitar practice. When we move on again I won't forget this place, but there'll be something new happening. It's a lovely way to live, for us anyway, and you can accept leaving stuff behind because of what's coming up ahead.

(Actually I reckon that all of us would soon be locked up in a mental home if we had to stay in one place forever!)

I hadn't ever before gone back to a site alone though, and when I cried that day, looking over the green sea, I think I was crying because all that energy and love we had, left so little impression behind. Which is right and the way it's meant really, isn't it?

Stefan thought it was all for Silver Wind and said, 'We *will* find her.'

We didn't, though. Not then. There was *nothing* on the site left by her, nothing at all, in fact. Maybe I'd hoped for a message or something, I don't know. Stefan was impressed at how tidy we'd been, which just shows how the wrong idea even gets to clever and cool people.

I walked round the edge of the grassy table and tried to think which way Mum would choose to walk . . . at dawn. I thought of her samples kit, but there didn't seem much interesting around—just the endless wheat and the plants that you get at the edge of fields, wild oats and stuff—so that didn't help much. Finally I chose one of the tumbling dry-stone walls that ran between the fields, more-or-less south-east towards a darker smudge in the distance that was probably a hill or ridge. She'd want to walk towards the sun as it appeared, I thought, so we walked that way too, alongside the wall, and with me telling Number 1 all about Mum as we walked.

Maybe I would make it as a sleuth after all.

The trouble was, however much I wanted to find some trace of her, to make me at least sure that this was the way she'd chosen, she wasn't the sort to go slashing a path with a stick or something. At one point I thought I'd found a footprint that could have been hers, but Stefan didn't think much of it. The ground was too hard for prints, really, after no rain for so long.

About halfway to the smudge, sweating in the sun, carrying his rollneck over his shoulder, Stefan said, 'I don't get the feeling we're achieving much here. Surely she wouldn't have come this far so early in the morning?'

Well, Silver Wind was a fast walker, and also I was quite happy being in the open again, away from the smoggy roof and walls of snarled-up Camberwell and the gloomy wooden furniture . . . but I supposed he was right.

I said, 'OK . . . let's go across at the edge of this field and back on another wall-line then.'

But in the end we found a much quicker route back to the car. Provided by a burly farmer, leaning on the wall where we'd planned to turn back, watching us with unfriendly eyes: we didn't see him till we were quite close, but he might've been watching us the whole time. I don't know.

He didn't bother with hello or anything, just said, 'You realize you're trespassing, eh?'

It wasn't really a question.

Number 1 tried his posh voice and charm. 'Oh . . . oh, are we? I'm awfully sorry! We thought this was the path, next to the wall here, do you see? Got a bit lost, I'm afraid. If you could just tell us the best way to get off your land . . . '

'Path!' The farmer spat messily against his side of the wall and looked at us like we were insects. '*I've* never seen no path like that and I doubt you 'ave neither! Here . . .

get in and I'll *show* you the best way off my ruddy land. Take you back to your ruddy car, to make sure, I will. You 'ave *got* a car somewhere?' He spat again, muttered *'Path!'* and jerked his hand to sign that we should go further along the wall. Over the top we could see the roof of a Land Rover or something and I realized there was actually a lane where the farmer had been standing.

He'd already stalked off towards the vehicle, so we found ourselves going after him till we came to a gap in the wall and a gate. Farmer Spit stood waiting for us, leaning on the red-earth-dusted bonnet, and we saw as we went through to his side of the barrier that there was also a nasty-looking dog, scarred and watery-eyed and untrusting of people.

Stefan tried again, but sounding a little less confident than before. 'Really, it's very kind of you . . . but there's no need, you know. We can just walk up this lane—if that's OK with you?—until we get back to the road. Must be quite simple from here.'

He tried a faint smile, but Farmer Spit just ignored him and heaved open the passenger door.

'Go on . . . get in!'

So we got in, and guess who ended up squeezed into the middle with the stoating dog?

'All right, now . . . where're you parked up, eh?'

Before Stefan spoke, I butted in and described the bit of ground where we'd camped. (I didn't want to spend too long near those teeth!) But I made it sound like it was difficult for me to remember, like we'd just seen the grass-table in the wheat sea today, because he must already be wondering if I was one of those *ruddy hippies* who'd been staying on his land and I didn't want him any more peed-off than he was already! Don't think it worked, though: he looked at me properly for the first time and said grimly, 'Oh . . . *there*. Yes, I know where you mean all right.'

And we went bouncing off down the lane, the dog slobbering on my knee while it growled. Poor thing probably got beaten.

A neat white sign at the end, facing for people going the other way, said that we'd been on Rook Rise Farm. Then we turned left onto the road and made our way back to the E-type in a big circuit. I thought the yellow car might impress the farmer, but he didn't pay any attention to it, except as a way to get us off and away from the land he thought was his.

He said: '*Now* then . . . *I* don't see no ruddy sign about no path anywhere here, do you? No, because there isn't one, see? Well, when there *is* a sign, you come right on back and have a wander!'

I think he was making what he thought was a joke because he grinned, but without any real laughter.

We got out of the Land Rover and Stefan unlocked the E-type, but I just *had* to ask the farmer about Silver Wind. 'Please, sir . . . have you perhaps seen anyone else on your land in the last few days? A woman . . . long dark hair . . . '

'Oh, *that's* what it is, is it? Well, I've had the ruddy police asking me all that already . . . not that I can see what it is to you, young scruff!'

I could feel the first prickles of anger. Maybe the dog sensed it in me because he growled from his place next to his master, so I caught hold of myself like Troll and Mum would have done, and decided to be sensible!

'She's my mother.'

Nothing changed: he just didn't care.

'She could be the ruddy queen: if I found her on *my* land I'd help her off it sharpish, just like I've done with you. No exceptions. *I* don't want my ruddy wheat trodden flat or full of crisp packets and Coke bottles. *And* no, I haven't seen your ruddy mother.' His nastiness suddenly stepped up a gear, like he'd reached the end of his patience (!!!) or something. 'Now *eff off*!'

'Eff off yourself.'

Whoops.

I just couldn't help myself and the words were out. So was the farmer, out of his Land Rover and grabbing me by the scruff of the neck faster than I'd have thought he could. The dog came out too, of course, to join the fun.

'Someone ought to teach you some manners!' He had his face close to mine and was breathing sour old peppermint and smoke over me. Yuck! I wondered vaguely how violent he was likely to get, but luckily didn't get to find out. Stefan, who'd been getting into the car to wait for me, shot out again. He looked steadily at the farmer for an instant, then reached back in behind the seats. I had a brief vision of him bringing out a gun or something, turning out to be armed for his mysterious job in the Civil Service, but in fact he had a camera in his hands, one of those ones where the picture comes out straight away.

Before my attacker knew what was happening, Stefan had pressed the button. He took the picture as it came sliding out, held it up meaningfully to the farmer, and then pushed it firmly down the front of his jeans.

From being keyed up ready to give old Farmer Spit a good struggle for his money, I could suddenly feel the giggles coming on. It was such a perfect reaction to the problem. Troll and Silver Wind would have approved, and Stefan went up several points in my view too. The farmer himself took a bit longer to realize what Number 1 (playing for the Traveller Team!) had done . . . and then he didn't find it at all funny.

'Give me that ruddy picture! Now! Before I get my shotgun out!'

Stefan said, 'Of course. Just let my friend go and when she and I are sitting comfortably in our car, I'll drop the picture on the ground for you, out of the window. Much simpler than shooting us.'

Spit didn't like it, but did what Stefan said.

The twelve-cylinder engine fired beautifully, the photo got thrown out, and we accelerated bumpily off towards the road.

After a few minutes Stefan broke the silence. 'I think we should wrap it up for today. I've had enough excitement. What do you think, 99? We can always come back again tomorrow and have a nose around further west for your friends.'

I really *would* have liked to try now, but I thought it wasn't fair on him, so I said, 'OK, Number 1. Cool.'

When we were on the motorway and the London claustrophobia was back, catching at my throat, he spoke again.

'Unpleasant type, wasn't he, that farmer with nothing to do except threaten people?'

'Yeah. The land is for everyone anyway. You can't really own it.'

He glanced at me, maybe to see if I really meant that.

'Well, perhaps. Do you know the funny thing, though?'

'What funny thing?'

'That photo I gave him. It was of some sea lions at the zoo. I was there last week. The real one is in the glove compartment. You never know when you might need insurance . . . mmm?'

5

All through those two months last spring I kept thinking I'd got to the bottom of the drop. When Alice followed the white rabbit—oh yeah, I *can* read by the way, in case I didn't say that before—she at least hit the floor in the end and was able to start dealing with all the weird stuff that went with the new world. But I *never* seemed to get there, just kept on plunging down the hole.

Two things happened that same day, after Stefan had dropped me off and gone back to his own life. (He didn't say any more about going back down again to find my crew, which was about the only thing left for me, and I thought probably that was it, he'd had enough of my company and farmers and the police.)

The first thing was that Brenda had come to see Rose Payne and sold her a load of you-know-what about me being a special case so that the monitoring of my progress (as a foster child) would be done by her personally. They'd filled out more forms together and she, Brenda, was going to visit at least once every two days for a report 'until I'd settled in'.

What a thought!

I couldn't help telling Rose what I reckoned to that: 'Settled in! I don't believe the old cow! Mrs Payne, you're really lovely and if I was a proper foster child and all that it would be you I'd want, no doubt at all, but my mum's gone missing and I'm only supposed to be *here* until they find her. I'm not supposed to be stoating settling *anywhere*.'

She said, 'I know, Kez. I do know that. I don't want you not to get back with your mum. But . . . Stefan thinks we should go along with her for now. Act normal . . . you know. After your little trip today he . . . well, he seemed to think that you might be in some sort of danger or something.'

I could feel hairs going up on my neck. The thought of *me* being in danger, real danger, hadn't properly come to me before, I suppose. And Stefan had seemed cool, in control, not worried about anything too much. I guess I'd thought—still thought, maybe—that there was just some sort of anti-Traveller hassle going on . . . that they'd just seen a chance to stick me away from my own people and try and brainwash me a bit. Reclaim one crusty girl for a normal life in the dole queues of South London.

That's the kind of thing those people do, isn't it?

Rose was speaking again. She looked as troubled as me, the kind eyes doubtful. 'I mean, I've always found Mrs Cotterell a strange fish, it's true, and God knows she's irritating . . . *and* doesn't seem to give tuppence for half the children she places . . . but . . . *dangerous*? Oh well, listen, Kez, I know you won't be keen, but she wants you to start school. Here, that is, in Camberwell. On Monday.'

I don't think I should write what I said after that, and I think that it shows how sorted Rose is that she didn't bat an eyelid or get upset! Whoever got her into the fostering thing to start with gave ninety-nine kids a lovely present.

'I'm sorry, dear, but she said that school was a condition for you staying here. Said that you'd been in some sort of trouble before and she could get you put in a children's home if she thought it was needed. You know, a secure one, what they used to call borstal.'

Some sort of trouble. I saw again in one beautiful dreamy moment a heavy lump of steel and a shower of rainbow-coloured glass. Glass from a police car windscreen. Oh great Goddess, forgive me for my negatives not going as they should, but let me do the same with Brenda's car, every window. And then her house maybe.

But Alice didn't stop falling—was Brenda the White Rabbit, I wonder?—and there was more to come that evening, while Rose and I were watching TV.

The phone went and it was Stefan. Told us to watch the news on the other channel. Told *me* again to stay put, to go along with Brenda, even the school thing, and not to go back down to Basingstoke or anywhere near there, until he got in touch again.

'Soon,' he said. 'Certainly in the next two or three days. Then I hope to be able to tell you something.'

Rose went plumply to the ancient TV in her furry slippers and pressed the button. We had been watching something about King Alfred. A re-enactment of one of his campaigns, with lots of actors all in old warrior clothes hacking away at each other in some west-country marsh somewhere. Well, the first impression when the channel flipped over was that it was the same stoating thing we were seeing. Long-haired warriors crying defiance at the invader and all that. Only *here* the other half—the invader—were dressed in dark blue . . . and the long-haired warriors were having their homes broken up, or towed away, before *they* were put into white cars and vans and driven off. The warriors were my friends, my people, from the last site.

'Violence erupted today,' said the TV news guy, 'when police moved in to disband an illegal group of hippy Travellers who have been angering farmers, disturbing communities and, according to Scotland Yard, responsible for a string of burglaries and other crimes across the country from London to Bristol. A police spokesman, Superintendent Strong of Hampshire CID said: "We have given these people every chance to co-operate, but they chose to continue with their disruption and criminal activity. Indeed, a great deal of evidence was found during this raid, and I can confidently predict that there will be a number of convictions. Also, we will make it as difficult as possible for any members of this gang to return to their illegal lifestyle." Other news tonight . . . '

The way the thing was shown and with the smart announcer and all that, I suppose it was quite convincing if you didn't know the truth.

To me the lie shouted out.

Bastards!! Stoating bastards!

The only good thing about it, if it *was* a good thing, was that Troll wasn't there. All the people I knew and loved were there, even pregnant Krissy being pushed into a police car like I'd been, but still no Jake, obviously no Mum . . . and no Troll.

That *had* to be good news . . . didn't it?

Of course, I *was* pretty scared after that. Every instinct told me to dive for cover, to simply disappear for a while, but Stefan had said stay put and he wasn't dim. Along with Rose, who cared and was pretty much on my side despite the news lies, Stefan was all I had right now.

But as you've seen, I'm not so good at just sitting and

52

accepting stuff. So the next day, with three days to go until I was supposed to be in school, I got the bus back to the Elephant and went to see the mauve girl. Brenda had apparently been peed off that I'd been allowed to go out driving with Stefan 'when she's still in that crucial re-adjustment phase'—obviously she didn't know where!—but Rose was cool about me exploring a bit on my own, as long as I was actually there on show and submissive in the afternoon when Brenda would be making another visit.

The girl wasn't there but the bearded guy like a pirate was: the boyfriend who didn't bite. It's true that he had a bit of a wild look in his eyes, but he turned out to speak very softly, to be called Ron and to understand what I wanted. Since I couldn't get the lift down with them next week (Oh, *Goddess* I wanted to take it . . . to hit the summer festival circuit and leave behind the idiots from the system who were trying to squash me!) they would take a message for me instead. If Troll *was* OK and still free and unhurt, there was a good chance he'd be doing the festivals himself. Like an animal in danger, or hurt, goes back to its own kind. And even if they didn't manage to get my message to him through the network, there were other friends of Troll and Silver Wind out there somewhere.

'No sweat,' Ron the pirate said. 'We'll put the word out. Here, I'll write down the mobile number so you can get us . . . and you give me yours.'

He was faraway, like the mauve girl. Totally sorted, though.

I got the bus back 'home', where Rose wanted me to give her some ideas for what a vegetarian would or wouldn't eat (to take my mind off things?) and where I'd have to think myself into being all balanced and accepting and no trouble for Brenda . . . and just to hang around till Monday and school. The thought of *that* made me scream. Did I tell you that I'm not really a big fan of school? But unless Stefan phoned that was about all I could do.

Of course, I yogaed and breathed and all that, without my inner self really having much chance of moving towards peace right now, and when I walked into the local comprehensive on Monday (no phone calls!) I was as wound up as ever.

Not such a good way to start.

'Oh yes, Kez Harrison. Is that right? Mrs Cotterell told us you'd be along this morning. Didn't Mrs Payne bring you?'

'No.' She'd wanted to and told Brenda she would, but I preferred bringing myself.

'All right. Now, Kez, perhaps you could just sit there a moment as we have to do a few forms for you, to fill in the gaps. First of all, could you tell me what Kez is short for?'

The trouble with forms, I've learned since all this started, is that they're just full of questions that don't apply to Travellers. I gave the woman the real answers, but she ended up putting me down as a runaway or something, 'home unknown'. And for my education she wasn't interested in what I knew, only in what bits of paper I had (none of course!). She even started writing down that my name was Catherine, which I suppose was a guess or just an easy lie for the form, after I told her that I was just Kez, not short for anything. If you don't match the stuff in the forms, you're *nothing* and they can do what they want with you. Like you don't even exist.

This was my second big form-filling session in just a few days and I was already pretty sure that they weren't for me.

'Oh, and the hair, Kez. I'm very sorry, but that will have to be . . . tamed a little. We're quite easygoing here, but we do have some minimum requirements.'

I counted backwards from eight, seeing each number in 3D in my mind, concentrating on colours and shapes, and kept silent. There was no way that my hair was going to be messed around. To be honest now, I reckon that with everything about my life blown away in less than a week, the hair and the stud and all that became more important to me, almost like a flag or something. Maybe a battle flag.

Mad grin.

The class I was put in had thirty-three other kids, white, black, and Asian, none looking like me. I was used to quite a lot of hassle in other schools I'd been in, but here I wound up as a good diversion from some of the normal gang warfare that had been going on before.

Crusty. Tramp. Hippy slag. Beggar. Alien. Why don't you take a bath?

By the end of day one I'd retreated even further from my path to enlightenment, got myself marked down as a troublemaker, and earned a little respect by 'sorting out' a leader of the hard white girls called Debbie.

'Not a very good day, dear?' Rose asked, trying not to look at the congealed blood on my lip.

'No, not very. The class teacher was OK though.'

Stefan didn't call, the news didn't have anything else about 'illegal hippies', nobody tried to do anything 'dangerous' to me and I burned away with frustration as the days went past. I was so frightened for Mum: I started getting nightmares about her. On the Wednesday I imagined Ron the pirate and the mauve girl (Hannah) packing up their van and hitting the roads away from this scummy, choking mess of a place and had to skip school for a morning to straighten my head.

Brenda Cotterell was there, hovering around my days, a sour old bitch who'd never lost her puppy fat or her spite . . . and in my dreams she was a kind of bloated fiery demon, wishing me harm, loving the hurt she made. Then other times I wondered why I was imagining all those things in her. Was she really so bad? I kept myself quiet for her visits, didn't show her anything to worry her. It didn't change the thing that somehow we were natural enemies and both knew it. How can you hide that stuff?

The day after I missed the morning at school she came there to see me and the class teacher so we could all talk about what stoating *goals* I could set myself . . . apart from getting Silver Wind and my friends and home back, that is. Something to use up any rebellious energy I had was what they meant, I suppose.

Miss Gibbons, the teacher, said, 'The trouble is, Mrs Cotterell, that it's getting rather late in the school year and the pupils are all nearing the end of Key Stage 3. Most of them will be doing exams this summer before moving on to GCSE choices. It's rather an odd time to be joining us, you see: not very motivating for poor Kez, I expect.'

Mrs Cotterell's shiny rat eyes said that Key Stage 3 meant about as much to her as it did to me . . . she just wanted me put to work! I wouldn't have been surprised if she'd suggested peeling potatoes in the school kitchen or scrubbing out the toilets maybe. Not that I would have much minded either of those. Believe me.

'But there *is* one thing going on at the moment,' Miss Gibbons continued, 'in English and Communication, which is a sort of life skills thing I do with the class. Either in pairs or singly, the pupils are to prepare a presentation on an aspect of modern life. They have to negotiate the topics, do any research themselves in their own time, and in class we work on presentational technique and that side of things. Now, I'm not sure without checking which pupils haven't submitted a subject yet, or are in need of a pair, but perhaps . . . '

'OK,' I said, 'but I'll do mine alone.'

Miss Gibbons looked doubtful. 'Are you sure? You wouldn't find it easier to get up and speak to the class with someone else? Being so new to us, that is.'

'Alone . . . please.'

Brenda was fuming. 'Are you really *sure* this is the sort of thing that will . . . *direct* her : . . or perhaps you would say *involve* her, in school life? It sounds like it could be a recipe for more truancy, or laziness.'

Then someone else suggested something.

This talk was in the classroom, at lunchtime, round the teacher's desk. The other kids were all outside or at lunch, but one boy I knew vaguely by sight was sitting at the back, reading. All I knew about him up till now was that he was tall and slim, black, and much quieter than most of that lot. Also, he wasn't ever part of the classroom wars.

And this was Joe! So I might as well just start calling him 'Joe' right now, and not 'the boy' or something.

Joe looked up from his book and said, 'Why don't she do a presentation on living like she do?'

Brenda hadn't even seen that there was another person there and, just for a change, wasn't happy! (Poor woman, always trying to control so much stuff that didn't want to be controlled!) 'What's this boy doing here, Miss Gibbons? This should be a confidential discussion, you know.'

Miss Gibbons shrugged. 'Oh, that's just Joe. He usually works in here, or reads, at lunchtime. He's very sensible, don't worry.'

'Sensible maybe . . . ' Brenda started again, unbelievingly, but then Joe just calmly repeated his question.

'Why don't she do a presentation on living like she do? Shut up some of them others. Make 'em think, right?'

Then he got up and calmly walked past us out of the room. I noticed he walked a bit lopsidedly like there was something wrong with his leg. As he reached the door he turned back for a moment and said, just to the room in general, '*Directing* folks ain't no good.'

When he'd gone Brenda was *more* irritated than ever, Miss Gibbons was soothing and I think quite into Joe's idea for my presentation, and I was smiling at this boy Joe's back. He was sharp and he seemed to have seen the hidden stuff (about Brenda!) quickly, which always pleases me.

So thanks to Miss Gibbons, the professional, and Joe, who had a bit of sense, I did end up agreeing to do something for the class on what it was to be a Traveller.

The funny thing is that it *did* end up getting me 'involved' and using some of my energy, just like Brenda wanted. In fact, with all that had happened to me and was going on happening, I finished up caring more about this chance to think about what I was and where I was going—and to stand up and say it—than about anything else that ever happened at any school I've ever been to.

Sort of like finding myself and getting strong again.

A rebirth.

Stefan didn't phone in the end—he turned up himself.

It was maybe seven on Sunday morning, already ten whole days after going to Basingstoke, and he was grim and starving, so I got him something to eat in Rose's kitchen while he talked. (She'd gone to church—is that why he came then?)

'I've got to be in Birmingham of all places at ten, Kez, so just listen first, OK?'

'OK,' I said, but thought: *Help, what's coming? What's he going to tell me?* That morning, just like all the rest, I'd been awake early and hollow inside from not knowing about Silver Wind.

Bursting-with-life Silver Wind.

But Stefan said, 'First: I have no news of your mother yet. Or your friend. I'm sorry, Kez . . . ' And the hollowness jumped and sprouted even bigger inside me. 'Second: I do not believe that the police have any genuine evidence against the rest of your . . . um . . . group, and I suspect that their aim was just to break them up and separate them. Your friends have actually been taken to many different police stations around the country: *why* is not yet clear. However, bearing that aim in mind I doubt that there will be any convictions; perhaps not even prosecutions. Third . . . well, the third thing is connected to the second: whatever the aim is of those people involved in this matter, like perhaps Mrs Cotterell or Sergeant Gregg, it is not primarily to do with any of you. Of that I'm one hundred per cent certain—and that may be some comfort.'

Of that I'm one hundred per cent certain. That strange piece of ice in me wondered if you had to talk like that to be in the Civil Service, while the rest of me plunged right on down past where Alice's marmalade should have been.

'However, I'm equally certain that it is something large and well organized and that anyone creating problems might well be in danger. I can only guess that your group *did* create a problem of some sort, probably unknowingly, possibly to do with your mother. I'm sorry to sound so vague, but . . . '

Stefan paused and went to the sink to splash water on his face. He looked tired and edgy. Quite different from the guy who'd charmed me when we met only last week.

'Finally, fourth . . . fourth and perhaps worst of all is that I'm reasonably sure that they—whoever *they* are—know about our visit to Basingstoke and that I am involved . . . on the wrong team, shall we say. Perhaps that policeman to whom you handed all that rock star rubbish was *not* as stupid as he looked. I don't know. I've even wondered about the farmer, though I'm probably seeing ghosts. You know, he made very sure he took us back to the car himself. To have a look at the registration, do you think? Or is that just paranoia?'

Not much good asking me. I was outclassing him for paranoia.

He broke off again, leaning on the draining board, looking out the kitchen window at Rose's sad little patch of grass and concrete. I wondered again what *his* story was, whether he'd kicked a ball around the back there in shorts once . . . or just sat on the steps and cried, perhaps on the day he'd arrived. Still not a good time to ask, though. He turned back to where I was burning his eggs and said:

'Our mysterious "they" are on to me, Kez, aware of me, I'm sure of it. I've found so many ways blocked; so many possibilities closed that would usually be open. And that means that whatever this *is* goes high, perhaps even to the top. Do you understand what I mean by that?'

'Well, sort of.' Meaning 'no'.

'Do you know where I've just come from? Blasted Hamburg. They sent me three days ago and I only left to come back yesterday afternoon—driving through the night. Before that it was Glasgow. The day after our trip. And now two days in Birmingham. All piddling little jobs that some other idiot could sort out, but suddenly they want me everywhere.'

I had to ask *something* to get a handle on Stefan's world, so like an idiot said, 'Are you a . . . secret agent?'

Stefan smiled for the first time. 'No. Not an agent. I thought I told you before: you shouldn't listen to Rose's fantasies! No, just a bureaucrat in the Civil Service, I'm afraid. Certain parts of my work are confidential, but only because they're to do with things the public shouldn't know about yet, like planning new roads or deals that are being negotiated with friendly governments. Nothing too shocking or immoral. And no, the car does not have an ejector seat or an underwater function!'

OK. I know. So what would *you* have thought?

I probably had no idea about Stefan's world, like he didn't about mine. The *system*, that's what it is. People you never meet making decisions: the government and all that. And the ones behind them: people like Stefan maybe. When you're out under a clear sky, under the stars, it all seems mental, not important or real at all. Except when they want to stick a road through some lovely bit of forest or something. Then it seems evil.

It was difficult knowing that I liked Stefan but that he was also part of that grey face. Surely they couldn't all be as cool as him, or why would we be in the stoating state we're in?

He ate his burnt eggs and drank tea and left again. Don't go back west, he said again. Don't do anything to get Brenda's attention. Don't make a fuss. Wait for more from him. Be good.

'Remember that you're one little girl right in the eye of perhaps a very big storm,' he told me, over the brief buzz of his battery razor and then the throaty roar of the E-type as he turned the key with his free hand, tossed the razor onto the spare seat and aimed that sleek canary nose at Birmingham.

The 'little girl' cleared away the dishes and then went up and did yoga, and spent the day not thinking about the storm but instead how she could explain about the clear skies to the other kids in her class, kids who'd grown up in the smog and with the *system* and cable TV and no trees.

Like I said before, the whole thing'd got me finding again who I was. Who Number 1 was was his own problem.

6

'*Hair*, Miss Harrison! I thought you were going to get it cut.'

'I *can't*: it's my religion, miss.'

The poor teachers didn't really have enough info on all the kids in the school and the different religions and languages and how they lived at home, although they did try their best. Some bits were easy and obvious for them like giving the Muslims a place to pray five times a day . . . but there were so many other needs that when you were in trouble about something you said, 'It's my religion.' Even the teachers sometimes smiled.

(There were other set excuses, of course, but it took me a while to understand half of what those kids said, with their Londonspeak thing, whatever it's called. Toughnut Debbie got detention for having a go at me that first day. She pulled a face at Miss Gibbons and said, 'You're 'aving a bubble, miss. That's well extra, that is!'

and no one would tell me then that *bubble* was *bubble bath* was *laugh*.)

The mix of religions and needs was good for me because there was always OK vegetarian food at lunch, although most of the kids ate nothing but crisps and chips and Mars bars and Coke.

Yuck.

Me having the rice dish or the pasta was another good reason for them to think I was a nutty alien, and it didn't matter that *they* were all different from each other. The one thing that they all knew was living in a house and in London and that was enough of a difference to make the hassles continue.

I half dreaded the presentation thing, which was coming up in only just over two weeks, trying to make them see that there was more to being a Traveller than not washing! But also, like the cold mornings in winter, it was something that would make me know I was alive . . . and so it had a good side. *Also* it was something to think about that wasn't Mum.

Joe was the only one at school I got to know well.

When I smiled at the space where he'd been when he left the room that first time, I felt a bit of a prickle up my back; and next time I saw him, and he smiled at *me* there was even more of the prickle, or a little delicious shiver. A *connection*. We were in one of the school corridors, stinking of disinfectant and polish or whatever the poison is they always put on everything in big schools. I was running and late for registration, but when I saw Joe limping along ahead of me—also late but not hurrying—I ran up next to him and started walking with him. I was going to say thanks for having a little go at Brenda before but he turned to see who it was, and smiled, and I found myself smiling right back and not saying anything after all. From what he told me afterwards he also had the prickle, though I didn't know that at first.

The only thing I did say, just as we got to the classroom, was: 'I'm Kez.'

And he said, 'I know that.'

Romantic stuff.

If you want to know was it love or what, then I couldn't say back then, and I don't think I'm even sure right now, a year later. Maybe it's not always helpful to try and find a name for something. Name something special like that and you might find you've lost it.

Anyway, Joe was quiet and not part of the general aggro, and he walked a bit stiffly, and all those things came from having been a drugs delivery boy after school for his bad-news older brother. Lots of the kids at that school were caught up in stuff like that, which was a real shock. Even little ones, just out of primary school, with runny noses, hopping on their bikes at four o'clock and going off to do errands for guys with guns in XR3is and BMWs with tinted windows. Coke and crack and speed and acid and ecstasy. A million miles from the grass that some of our lot smoked sometimes.

(All those police they used to break up our sites should have come and waded into that lot, but like I said, these people had guns and used children.)

It turned out that Joe's injury was not that unusual.

'You see that kid there?' he asked one day. We were sitting at lunch, still very new to each other and with loads to find out, but already getting hassles from the other idiots. I'd finally got up some courage to ask Joe about his leg. 'That kid there is sixteen and got just one eye he can see with. One good eye and the other . . . well, you'll see it, girl. That kid lives right near me and his eye got shot out by a man who already'd made a whole, big pile of money from him. An' he got shot due to another guy, another just the same, making him do something to get even *more* money, which the first guy, big man that he was, thought was moving in on *his* ground.'

. I wouldn't have guessed that Joe could get fired right up like this. He'd put down his fork and although he wasn't shouting I could feel his anger coming through, strong and quiet like he was about most things.

I hadn't really caught on what he meant, of course, except that he wasn't angry with me, thank the Goddess . . . but he hadn't even properly started yet and he spelled it out for me.

'Drugs, girl. Drugs. *That's* what messed up Mikey's eye and my leg. *Hey, Joe*, my brother says to me when I'm eight. *Hey, Joe. Hey, boy. You wanta do something for me, lil brother? You want some chocolate, some new trainers, boy?* My *brother* call himself Rocket, Kez, though his mother named him better than that. So my brother Rocket says: *Hey, Joe-boy . . . just get on your bike, give this parcel to a man you'll find in a place I'm gonna tell you about, lil bro, and then we'll get you some cool Nikes, huh?* And lil bro did it, did it for four years until my leg was done.'

There was lots more and Joe was pretty bitter like I would've been too. Like the older kid Mikey, he had been shot.

I suppose you could think that Joe was lucky that he just got shot in the leg, so that he had some metal pins there now. Or maybe not so lucky, because before that running had been his thing. He'd been really good, supposed to be up for a place in a national team, ready to lift himself out of Peckham and delivering drugs. When his brother made him do the drop-offs he used to use it to train, jogging round to see the dodgy types in his tracksuit and trainers. The most common thing, Joe said, was for people to get hurt because of rival gangs, all jealously trying to muscle in on the market, but *he* just got shot by the guy he was supposed to see for his delivery. The guy was speeding and twitchy and when Joe appeared running towards him in the drizzly evening he freaked out.

Like I said, all this was new to me, and maybe (hopefully!) it is to you too. The whole story took a couple of days to come out too, and I think maybe didn't get shared easily.

'But why did you agree to do it?' I asked Joe naively.

He said, 'No one agrees. These kids, you think they agree? They grow up to it and in it, like me. They get beaten and beaten if they say no. It was my brother for me but it could be the father, the mother. How say no then, girl? And not eat. And get beaten. Then when they do it they get cash, fifty quid maybe.'

Joe's brother had been a boy on a bicycle once for his dad, then he graduated and used Joe himself. But now Joe had broken the circle. When he got out of hospital his brother, Rocket, thought he was going to have his delivery boy again. 'You'll like to move again after that damn bed, man!' he'd said, but Joe refused and his mum had surfaced from alcoholic nothingness long enough to back him up.

Lucky Joe.

Of course I never got to see Joe before the shooting, so I can't be sure, but I reckon he probably did change a lot. It made him grow, I think, or get wise . . . but then he'd probably rather still have two good legs instead.

One thing was certain: his brother, who worked now for some other bigger fish called Sweet-Talk (of all things), was permanently angry with Joe for what he reckoned was a betrayal, and was always trying to get him back into the game. Like half these guys, he'd picked up a coke habit himself, was mostly out of control, and was starting to get in debt with Sweet-Talk.

'He's going to be found in the river soon,' Joe said, and despite everything I could see that he really cared.

Between Joe and Rose, I got to know Camberwell and Peckham and up to the Oval and didn't feel quite as bad about the place, although I could still hardly breathe.

Waking up next to the wheat and with space all around became just something that had happened in my past. It was only Mum I cared about, and *that* ache got worse each day, waiting for news.

Rose had lived there all her life and knew loads of people and I started to know them too. Shopkeepers and neighbours and types you just bumped into on the street. Goddess, I was starting to be a London girl! Of course with my dreads I was easy to recognize for *them* too, so I got quite a few 'Hello's when I walked up to school in the mornings. There were even a couple more of Rose's gang of ex-foster kids still living locally. The best of those was Number 64, who was really called Denise and ran a tiny flower shop up on the main bus route near all the kebab and curry places. She said I could work there on Saturdays if I needed some money, so I said yes please and started the next weekend. Denise was scrawny and birdlike and kind and had been knocked about by her dad till Rose got her. When Joe came by that first Saturday to see me, he and Denise hit it off at once—two survivors of horrible families; both tough and sad and coping—so it got to be a place where Joe and I spent lots of our free time.

Like I said, I was almost doing what Brenda wanted and settling down to some kind of life here.

Almost.

I would have cheerfully ditched the lot of them to get back to the bus and Silver Wind. Well, that's what I thought. But then somehow they all got to be part of the story too.

For almost two weeks after the Sunday visit Stefan was out of touch. I was stoating freaked out, living this other life, not knowing what was happening under those other skies. I got Rose to give me his number, his mobile too, and broke his rule by trying to call him: but the flat phone just rang endlessly and the mobile made an unobtainable bleep.

Even Rose, who didn't really know what was going on (I hadn't told her about Stefan's last visit) was worried. 'He usually rings me up at least once a week, you know,' she said. 'Just to see how I am. He's always been the best of them all at things like that. Very considerate.'

I'd already decided what I wanted to do. 'Is it OK if I take the bus to try and see him at his flat? After school tomorrow, maybe? It's not a Brenda day.'

Stefan lived somewhere in Chelsea, which meant nothing except I knew it was the other side of the river and posh, but even if it took me two hours to find the place, at least I would be *doing* something. The alternative was sitting on the floor with my back against the wardrobe mirror, looking at the nearly empty paper that was meant to be my presentation. Next Tuesday I would have fifteen whole minutes with whatever bunch from the class had bothered to turn up. So far, my only sentence was: *I am a Traveller, I am clean and I live under the open skies.* As soon as I got past that I just ended up thinking too much and getting too wound up and just wanting everything to go back to before Silver Wind went walking in the dawn.

The class would think I was having a bubble.

Rose said, 'All right, dear, you go and see Stefan and we can put our minds at rest. But if you take a friend I'll be happier, just in case you get lost or anything.'

Of course I was going to take Joe. I was meeting him later in the evening down on Peckham Common, so I'd ask him then. (Today *was* a Brenda day—snarl!—which was why I wasn't already out.)

But then things worked out differently. I got to meet Rocket.

I took the bus down to Peckham, which I'd already done a couple of times before, and met Joe OK and we started walking round the edge of the common, talking and stuff . . . and then suddenly there was a long car horn and a blood-red BMW stopping level with us. Or more screeching-and-sliding than proper stopping really, and with the horn held down all the time. And this big idiot got out just like you'd expect and slammed his door for no reason and came arrogantly and aggressively across the grass towards us.

'Rocket,' Joe said quietly. I'd already guessed.

His brother liked open shirts and coloured leather jackets and lots of fat gold jewellery and he wasn't used to having to walk on grass. Also, he spoke like he walked and looked angry all the time and couldn't speak without two out of every three words starting with 'f'.

Why didn't any of that surprise me?

If you cut out the abuse and the all the 'f's, what he said, sorry . . . what he *shouted* was something like: 'Hey, boy. *Hey*, little boy. What are you doing here, boy? What are you doing here with this tramp, hey, boy? *This* what you into now, boy, is it? Can't find no clean girls? *I'll* get something for you, you little ****. Just ask *me* if you need something, you little ****. But don't waste no time with *this* trash off the street. *Hey*, boy . . . I'm *talking* to you.'

With the abuse it went on for maybe five minutes. A one-way river of nastiness with Rocket firing his tongue at his brother like it was his piece, worked up with coke and self-love into rage, veins swelling out on his neck and forehead. Not a word or a look to me. Joe just stood there and took it. I thought Rocket was going to slap him during the blast, but then Joe was almost as tall as his brother, and was strong. Maybe what really made Rocket angry was knowing that Joe wasn't going to be little brother for much longer.

Afterwards, when Rocket had stalked and slithered angrily back to his car and roared off, Joe put his arm round me and said sadly:

'I'm sorry, girl. Don't mind what he says. He doesn't know nothing. *I* think you're beautiful. I just get frozen . . . frozen up inside. I can't speak to that man when he's like that, though he's my brother. My brother! I can't do *nothing*.'

For the first time he held me against him, so that I could feel his warm body and he kissed my ear. Sweet. I think he felt he'd let me down or something. I didn't—and don't—mind words, though, and was only hurt for him. Worried too.

Later, as we walked back up to the bus stop, with Joe's arm round me, he said, 'That man is going down, Kez. And he know it. He messed too much with Sweet-Talk and he's going down. That's why he said those things.'

'Is there anything you can do?' I asked.

'No. Not one thing. I'm fourteen, Kez. Sweet-Talk's going to kill him one day soon.'

There was something *I* could do, though, which was not drag him off to Chelsea and plunge him right into all *my* problems. Joe had enough hassle right now.

There was only one other person I could think of, so I asked Rose when I got back in. 'Does Denise know Stefan? I mean, do they get on? Would she come with me tomorrow, d'you think?'

'Ask her, dear. Yes, of course they know each other.'

So I asked her and she said yes.

Falling, falling, falling.
  No ground.
  Not like Alice.

Stefan lived in the basement of a massive house, in a semi-circular row of expensive-looking houses, which Denise said were probably Regency.

Denise was short and slight and couldn't ever keep still for two seconds and probably felt as alien here as I did, in her scruffy old checked shirt from the flower shop.

'Down the back, I think it is. Only been here once, but I think there's a little street running round the back. A mews they call it. All the gentry used to keep their horses and carriages there, so now they use it for garages. And old Stefan's got some steps down to his place round there.'

Falling, falling.

I saw it at once when we turned into the little street, the mews, along the back. An ugly black lump, with bright red and white tape round it, and a bored policeman leaning against the nearest garage, reading a magazine.

The long, low shape was impossible not to recognize. A tiny spot of canary paintwork shone out from the lumpy black in the sinking sun. No more 90-mile-an-hour blasts of country air.

Even before we'd taken a step into the little street I'd grabbed Denise's arm and wheeled her round again and away. It was just reflex.

'What's up, Kez?'

'What's up is that that was Stefan's car, his Jag. Burnt.' I was white, shaking I think, and wanted to get away from there, most of all away from the police guy. For all I knew he'd probably lit the match.

Denise brought me to a stop and studied my face and I guess she could see I wasn't kidding, so she didn't question it. She looked a bit shaken herself, but she said, 'Neighbours. Come on. Let's ring a few bells round the front. One of the neighbours'll know what happened. Unless you reckon Stefan might still be in his flat? We could try that first.'

I shook my head. 'We don't want to be seen. Especially me 'cause of the hair. And especially not by that policeman outside Stefan's.'

Denise thought a moment. 'OK. You think you might get recognized, so you go and sit in that bit of park we passed a few minutes ago, and I'*ll* ring some doorbells by myself. Starting with Stefan's.'

'No, Denise! Not his, please! Really. Just the others. At the front.'

'OK,' she shrugged, a bit puzzled. 'Not Stefan's then. I'll come and find you in twenty minutes . . . and then I think you should tell me what's going on.' She walked off to the first huge house front, and I got out of there.

'No more tea, Rose. Please don't fuss, I'm quite all right. All of you. It's just a scratch, as they say in films. I don't need the last rites.'

Stefan wasn't making a big deal of it, but he certainly didn't *look* great, weakly trying to protect his cup from Rose's hovering pot. The neat white bandage around his head went well with his skin.

When we'd finally tracked him down, thanks to his neighbours, at a dingy place called St John's teaching hospital, they'd mentioned 'concussion' and keeping him in for a night or more. Seeing two friendly faces he'd got focused enough to lose the nurses and head outside with us to find a taxi.

'Stories later,' he'd said weakly, huddled in his jacket, so I spent the journey letting Denise in on all the fun I'd had since losing Mum while he dozed and shivered.

Of course at Rose's place he was her little boy again. No choice. Denise and I—hanging around and getting in the way—were a bit amused and also itching to get all that stuff over so we could hear what had happened to him and the Jag . . . but when he was finally allowed to talk, there wasn't much.

'I'd just got back. A couple of days' break. Popped in to the flat to change and have a quick wash, pick up the post, you know, and then I was going to come on down here . . . to make sure *you* were OK, Kez! The only damned time I've been home in weeks! For various reasons I'd already decided it was best not to stay at the flat, or to use the phone to speak to you here. A bit paranoid, perhaps, but I was congratulating myself on being extra careful. *Now* though . . . ' He tailed off gloomily for a second and sipped tea. '*Now* I'm inclined to think we haven't been nearly careful enough. A situation that I will rectify first by seeing my solicitor tomorrow morning and letting him have a tape I've made with any information and guesses to date. You know . . . in the event of my death and all that.'

Denise said teasingly, 'Oh yeah, sure, Stefan, and I'll do the flowers. Stop being so dramatic and tell us about the car.' She looked frightened, though.

I felt just blown away. Was this really to do with me and Mum and the rest?

'Oh, the car. My beautiful car. Yes . . . as I say, I'd just popped in for a couple of minutes, so I didn't use the garage, just parked outside the back. I often do that. Locked it as usual and set the alarm. But when I got out again there were two chaps there with it, and they'd got the damned door open! Not a squeak from the alarm, mind you. And that's about it! One of them turned round and saw me and I was out cold on the road before I could even ask what they thought they were doing. When I woke up I was being put in an ambulance and the car was on fire. Several X-rays later the cavalry arrived and found me. Short, but not very sweet, as stories go.'

'But the car!' I said. 'Why torch the Jag? What was it, a warning or something?'

Stefan looked down at his hands, resting in his lap, and said slowly and carefully, as if it was a maths problem or something, 'I would say, Kez, that there are three possibilities. Possibility the first: they were just thugs, robbers, vandals, or undesirables of some sort and it wasn't my day. Unlikely, but just possible. Possibility the second: your idea of a warning of some kind, although not a very specific one. One thing bothers me with *that* idea: why open the car first if they wanted to burn it?'

Denise said thoughtfully, 'To start the fire inside first. To give it more chance to take hold. Also, you'd clocked them, so maybe the fire was just an afterthought, to get rid of fingerprints or something.'

'Yes, some of that may well be right. I don't believe the fire was the original or, at least, not the main intention here. Which brings us to possibility the third. The most unpleasant possibility and so, given what's happened to date, perhaps the most likely. These men *wanted* something. Not the car . . . those things are almost impossible to sell on, and not the stereo as they'd get a better one from the average Sierra! In fact on all counts any robber would do better to choose the Sierra. But there was one thing in there that they *might* possibly have wanted, if they really were in with the Sergeant Gregg brigade.'

We all looked blank. *My* brain didn't want to work at all.

Stefan said, 'At the hospital waiting for X-rays I made a list of everything that I kept in the car, everything I could remember anyway. Then it was easy to guess. When I held the finished list in my hand there was only one thing on it that somebody might think it worth trying to take away from that particular car. One thing that could . . . well, be seen as a threat maybe, if you had something to hide. Think about it, Kez.'

Rose and Denise were still lost, but I suddenly knew what it was.

'The photo. The photo you took of that farmer threatening me!'

I knew he was right. I felt it. The ice deep inside me now was no cool watcher: it came from knowing how far and accurately and brutally these people could reach. The police and the social services and now that farmer too, for some reason.

Stefan's insurance policy had been a bad idea after all.

7

Summer proper was here. The heat kept on growing and my skin was going brown. At school I was in trouble for wearing a Rose-provided short skirt and sleeveless top that didn't fit in with the 'accepted dress code'. Huh, big deal! In Camberwell and Peckham the air got thicker and nastier from the endless crawling lines of traffic, but out in the fields near Basingstoke the olive green wheat heads would be going yellow gold, probably about a month earlier than usual thanks to this weather.

Looking back, that must have been about our lowest point, though usually it's such a lovely hopeful bit of the year.

Stefan had been beaten up and lost his car. The number of people included in whatever stoating *thing* that was going on kept seeming to grow. Everyone from my normal life had been spirited away or lost to me in some way. Also, the presentation was coming up in a few days, and for some reason I cared enough not to blow it away, despite the rest. Also . . . *also*, just to cheer things up more, Joe didn't turn up at school the last two days that week and I had a bad feeling about that.

At the bottom of every thought was Silver Wind. My beautiful, sparkling mum. If that farmer was really part of 'it' (??!!) then maybe he'd actually done her some harm himself. I thought that he'd be able to harm. I didn't lose hope though. I'd persuaded myself that I'd know inside if she was dead or something.

The last blow was that Stefan 'pulling rank' on anyone in his mysterious job seemed about finished with. That's what he thought, anyway.

'I've rung in to the office and been told I have an appointment tomorrow with . . . a superior,' he said. 'And do you know? I've the strangest feeling I'm about to be made redundant.'

'We're being beaten all round, aren't we? Totally destroyed,' I said bitterly.

'Perhaps. Yes, perhaps we are, Number 99.' He looked knackered and past caring for the moment.

The next morning, the one after rescuing him from the hospital, he went off by taxi to see his Civil Service employers and 'make a few arrangements'.

'I'll be back some time over the weekend,' he said, 'when I've sorted out some other, safer digs and a car and all that. And when I get back, Kez, I think that you and I should have a long talk about that place where you were last camped. Try to remember anything, absolutely anything, about what you saw there . . . also, anything your mum or the others said. You know, it's true that we're being quite soundly beaten at the moment, but it's just possible that . . . um, the "enemy" shall we call them, have made a first mistake. If they hadn't broken into the car I wouldn't have given that photo another thought . . . but now I can't help feeling that the key to this thing is

78

back with your mum, and that farmer, or something down there. *I've* got a few ideas already on that score, but you think about it too, 99—as hard as you can—and see what you can come up with. And one more thing . . . be careful! Don't get into any strange cars or anything.'

After a night's sleep he still looked rough, but not so weak inside any more. It came to me that he'd lost a lot for me, maybe would lose everything. I thought he deserved a hug, so I gave him one.

'Thanks, Stefan. Thanks for all of it. You're lovely!'

Then I went off to school, where Miss Gibbons said, 'All set for Tuesday?'

'Well, sort of,' I lied.

With Joe not being there I almost walked out to spend the afternoon doing something more useful. I guess I was close again to giving in to what I'd wanted to do all along . . . get *out* of there and find some of my own people; maybe catch up with Ron and Hannah or something. School and the presentation and Brenda—down to a visit every three days now—could get stuffed.

But not Rose. Not Stefan. Especially not Joe.

They were my people too now. Try and shut yourself in a room and the gold-green fingers of the Goddess come and open the door.

OK, Stefan, I thought, one more week and then I disappear back to the fields and lanes and do things *my* way. Maybe Joe would even come with me!

I don't know if I really meant it or not. I think I was pretty frightened when I really thought about just going it alone and leaving the few friends I had. But I didn't want to die in a fire or something either and I was fed up, *suffocating*, with not being able to do anything useful.

Like I said, this was the low point. Then . . .

That Saturday evening everything changed again. Still falling. Falling, falling, falling . . . but something came along that made me think that the bottom might have a nice pile of squidgy leaves when I finally got there and not cold, hard stone after all.

I got a phone call from Troll!

'Go to a phone box and ring Ron in ten minutes.'

That was all he said, and then *click* and nothing else. Some hello-how-are-you-doing-Kez that was! But I couldn't help loving him for being better at the cloak-and-dagger thing than the rest of us! Maybe the first team were back in business? Maybe. I grabbed some flower shop money and my fleece and went to dial Ron's number . . . with the biggest, silliest smile you could imagine stuck on my face.

Tears too.

'Steady, Kezzie, steady! One question at a time, hey?' Even down the line I could hear his quick, explosive grin, appearing and departing in a gnat's blink. *I* was not keeping my cool, but he still made me wait for news. 'Look, why don't you tell me how *you* are first, and what's been going down since we got split up.'

So I told him, as quickly as I could, everything from going to make sandwiches at the police station to Stefan losing his car. The flower coins rattled down inside the phone, one by one.

I couldn't have bought anything better than this.

Troll listened without interrupting and said, 'Sounds like you have some good people with you, which is really great to hear. I was worried. More than that.' He didn't need to say. We both knew. He took a breath. 'OK, here's what you want to know. Yes, the police really *did* fool me that day. Had the van waiting at their pound, and then directions to follow the rest of the group. Told me you'd been taken on with a car going to monitor our little convoy. Oh sure, the directions were spot on . . . but when

I caught up and there was no Kez . . . I did some quickish thinking and decided I should be alone, leave the van and go back to dig for answers round Basingstoke. The day after the raid I managed to see Jake being moved. At five in the morning. I managed to follow. When they finally let him go, it was in York, after three days in custody, and he was rough. But he had a message from that WPC you'd talked to, so I knew that you were OK for the moment . . .'

He'd known I was OK. I'd had almost four weeks of not knowing that my message had got through. 'But why didn't you phone me *then*?!'

'Jake didn't have a number. Your WPC was frightened, he said. Just wanted to let us know you were safe. Said to keep our heads down. When I got back to Basingstoke I phoned to try and see her, but she'd gone off on holiday, so they said. Bastards. What else? Oh yeah, Jake had started back to meet up with the others by that point, then before he got there he heard about the second raid, so he came back. There didn't seem any point *two* of us hanging about, so I suggested he should hit the festivals and listen and ask around a bit. Which was how he got your second message . . . Cool thought, Kezzie. We reckon that there's a good chance that some of the others will find us like that too.'

I couldn't take it. I was crying freely again with still not knowing. 'But *Mum* . . . ? What about Mum?'

A small silence. 'Sorry. I don't know yet, Kezzie. Like you, I *feel* she's still OK: but I can't be sure. Since Jake went off to the fezzies I've been trying to find her, busking around Basingstoke a bit and taking another look at the site. But I don't have anything yet, nothing solid, even if I could make a fair guess where she's being kept. I've come down to see Magog for a while, to let everything chill while I think about it. At least now I've found you I can relax for a day or two. I reckon we've still got about a month before it all hits the fan, so you might be safest staying put like your friend Stefan said. Until I let you know, anyway.'

We'd done so well, but now he'd lost me totally. If this was the first team, I was on the subs bench. Back in the pavilion or whatever they call it. The only thing I could make out was he was in Glastonbury. Magog was the name of one of the trees at the foot of the Tor.

'Um, Troll dear . . . *what* is going to hit the fan? And *what* fan? You mean there's more stuff that hasn't happened yet?' Help!

He was almost amused when he spoke. I could hear his grin again, spinning down the line.

'Wheat, Kez. Think about wheat.'

And that's all he would say about that, though I begged for more. So I told him about Joe instead, and *his* problems, and then about school and the presentation.

Troll thought that the presentation was a stoating wonderful idea.

'Wow! What a chance to put the case for an alternative existence! Educate all those future police officers and employers and voters to the idea that we aren't useless scruffy bums.'

I was doubtful. 'Errr, maybe. But I don't think there'll be many from *my* class joining the police.' Like none. 'And anyway, I've only got one sentence so far and it's crap.'

'Look, Kezzie, I've gotta go. Battery's going on this thing. But call again tomorrow, same number, same time-ish. Bring paper. We'll talk about what you can say for this caper on Tuesday.'

What a hero!

When I let myself in, Rose said, 'You look bright, dear! Good news at last? Am I right in thinking my 99 will be moving on soon?'

'Yes, Mrs Payne. I got to speak to my mum's boyfriend.'

'I'm so glad, dear. But I'll be sad when you go.'

Me too, I realized. The Goddess's slender fingers kept the doors open.

'It won't be that soon.'

When I'd done my teeth and all that I was still pretty worked up, too much to sleep, so I sent myself on one of the meditation journeys you can do.

There's nothing strange about it, in case you're still thinking I'm a hippy nut. You just do the meditation bit, concentrating on the sound and feeling of breathing, and you sort-of lead yourself into imagining a scene. The better you can see and feel and smell it and imagine all the textures and everything, the better. You're on a boat, travelling across some water, it could be a sea or lake or just whatever you see. Then you land on an island. Again, you make it whatever comes to you or seems best. You walk across the island and come to a hill or mountain to climb. And up you go. With mine I usually find I'm going way up above cloud level, where the air is icy and crystal clear. At the top, there's some sort of hut or shack or bender and as you get close a person comes out of this and gives you a present. A box maybe, with something inside.

The point is, that you never know—really!—*what* you're going to get.

That Saturday night there was no box.

The person from the hut was Silver Wind, the first time it'd ever been someone I knew, and she put in my open hand three heads of wheat, ripe and hard and ready for the mill.

Only when I closed my hand, the wheat seeds were hollow, empty, useless.

8

Perhaps I'd better slow down a bit or this next part of the story is going to be as tangled as a plate of spaghetti, which is about what it really was with so many things going on at once and affecting so many people.

There's loads of bits I've missed out in getting all this down, by the way. The wodge of paper is already quite thick, though, and there's a lot more to come. If I wrote about all the time I spent with Rose or Joe or working in the flower shop with Denise I think I'd just have to give up! They're all beautiful people, but this is a story about not very beautiful things happening even if there was so much good in it.

I never realized the wodge would get so thick.

Stefan first, then. Stefan *didn't* get knocked about again or anything, but came back to see us on the Sunday like he'd said . . . driving an old Fiesta!

E-type Stefan in a rusty XR2i. I did *try* not to laugh. He was already pretty embarrassed

'All the garage could lend me while they see if there's anything to salvage from mine,' he said, standing next to his new wheels. It'd put out about as much noise as the Jag and brought me and Rose and half the neighbours outside to look.

I said, 'It looks a bit sad. Maybe I can do some paintings on it. How about a ladybird on a leaf gazing up at the moon? I've done that one before so I know I can.'

I wasn't really serious. Just teasing because of how he looked. But Stefan said irritably, 'No! No paintings! Stay away from this car!'

Rose made her usual steaming pot of tea while he told us his news.

He'd sorted out a room somewhere, seen his solicitor . . . and his boss. He still had a job, but only just.

'I've been damn well moved to a different section. I'm to do the co-ordinating for a pre-legislation study on pedestrian-bloody-crossings of all things. No security clearance of any kind. I get use of an office in Whitehall two days a week. The funny thing, if there *is* anything funny in it, was that he and I both knew *why* I was being moved to such a dead end, but neither of us could mention it in case we forced the other one's hand. Mind you, that's normal in the service.'

'So if you aren't in all that secret stuff any more, can you tell us who he is, this guy you had to see?'

Stefan was doubtful. 'Well . . . in theory I'm still bound by the Official Secrets Act. Just in case I tell the Chinese how many lollipop ladies we're using or something! Excuse me if I sound bitter. All right, I'll tell you this much. The man I saw on Friday was a government minister. I don't know how much backing he's got. But I do know that my chances of finding anything out now are effectively zilch. Even useful colleagues will spurn me like the plague when they hear I'm on my way down, by blasted express elevator.' He stood near the front room window, holding a cup of tea and looking out at his Fiesta. 'I wonder what the fairer sex will think of my new transport.'

Fairer sex! Goddess, what a stoating relic he was sometimes.

'They'll love it,' I said. Not as much as the Jag maybe . . .

He looked so down that I thought it was about time to cheer him up with the news that my mates were also on the case.

Wow. It worked in a big way.

'Wheat! You're sure he said think about wheat?'

He started almost hopping round the room, grinning like a madman.

'That's right. And that (I looked across to where Rose was sitting quietly doing some knitting and a Sunday crossword at the same time) the er . . . you know what . . . would hit the fan in a month.'

'Of course! Alleluia, of course! How could I miss it? So damned obvious! The harvest! They must be going to harvest in a month's time. *That's* why they haven't done us any serious harm. Just kept us out of the way and tied up for a while. But the photo . . . the photo I took was different! That was evidence perhaps . . . maybe even showed a bit of that crop in the background.' He stopped prancing about and frowned into space instead. 'I wonder . . . does that mean that after the harvest they'll leave us alone? The evidence will probably all be gone, but . . . '

My head was spinning. He was as bad as Troll.

'You mean that there's something dodgy about those wheat fields? About the plants themselves?'

And then light started to dawn.

Without wanting it, a picture came into my head. Silver Wind, pulling on jeans while it was still dark, slipping her sampling kit over her shoulder, wandering into the midst of a sea of wheat, gently separating wheat heads from stalks by torchlight as the first pink gathered in the east. And then? Panic rose up in me and caught at my throat. The next part of my picture was a burly farmer, an evil dog, coming just as silently into the wheat.

Somehow up to now I'd put it off, the knowing, the stark fear. Now it swallowed me.

I realized Stefan had calmed down and was watching me. Calm, Kez. White light all around to keep you safe, white light around Silver Wind.

I couldn't trust myself to ask about Mum, not yet . . . so I asked instead, 'What *is* it, then, that wheat? And who are *they*? Who's that farmer *with*?'

Rose looked up from her crossword. '*They* are the government I should say, dear . . . and I expect this is all to do with that genetic thing you hear so much about these days. What are they called? GMOs . . . that's it, GMOs. It would be nice if you could mess it all up for them. Can't think why I voted for this lot now.'

Great. Stoating great. For the first time since I'd been in that class more or less everybody had turned up . . . to hear me speak! Maybe there were no drugs to be delivered that day. I didn't know if I should be pleased or if they'd all come to throw the first stone. Or maybe just to see the crusty chick on display, like a circus.

Just about the only one *not* there was Joe, and I had plenty of mixed feelings about that too.

At least, thanks to Troll, I now had a head full of spinning thoughts ready to spew out, things that I knew anyway really, or should have known, but hadn't been able to get together until I got prodded in the right direction by my friend's clear words.

'I'm not going to write a script for you, though, Kezzie,' he'd said, 'I'll just give you some ideas and we can talk a bit about how you might want to do it. Deliver it, I mean. In fact, the first thing is that you shouldn't *have* a script at all. An audience don't want to be *read* to . . . they want to be talked to, communicated with. Give them a little slice of you. Use what you know. You're the expert on this subject after all!'

So I spent a day and a half preparing, deliberately using this challenge to shut out everything else for a little while . . . and at 2 o'clock that Tuesday, with a dry throat and an empty stomach and after yoga-ing over lunch in one of the chemistry labs, the expert got up and faced thirty or so bored, hostile faces . . .

. . . and tried to kick things off by being funny!

'I'd like to talk to you today about my experiences as a Traveller . . . ' I started, reading from a paper and speaking as woodenly and tonelessly as possible. At the word 'Traveller' I glanced up and saw thirty pairs of eyes going glassy and unfocused . . . *'BUT* . . . ' (everyone sat up as I slowly tore my page across, screwed it up and tossed it over my shoulder) ' . . . this story starts way before paper (so we'll do without that), way before cities, way before houses even.'

All right, I know . . . I'm blushing myself as I remember doing that; but it's true and it's important. I talked to them about how humans are really nomads, right from the start, from when we started spreading over the world from some African valley up to now, with the Native Americans, the Karimajong cattle herders in West Africa, the Semang and Boro hunter-gatherers and mobile farmers of South America, the Romanies in Europe . . . the list goes on and on. It's only a recent and new thing that we have to build things that last and leave a mark and scar the landscape. As Travellers, we believe in leaving as little trace as we can, 'cause if you leave a trace or a mark then you haven't had respect for the Goddess or the world.

That got us on to 'resources'.

'Go to the library or something,' Troll had said. 'Get some information on how much water and electricity and gas the average British house uses. Compare it with what you know we use ourselves.'

So Monday after school had been devoted to that.

I was amazed by the figures, but I don't think most of that lot in my class could have cared less. You can't blame them, either, with all the drugs and unemployment and crap TV. And this presentation wasn't mostly for the others, it was for me. I didn't want to lose them completely, though, so at the end I said:

'Last, people, whatever you think, I *do* wash.' Just like I said to you at the start of this story, because that's always the first thing, the very first, that people think about us.

Miss Gibbons said, 'Thank you, Kez, that was very interesting. Now, would anyone like to ask Kez any questions in the time we've got left?'

'Yeah, 'ooz yer 'airdresser, Kez?'

'What's it like wiv Joe then? 'E any good?'

'If it's so great in yer stinking caravan, what you doing 'ere then?'

And suddenly I was off the rails, off for the first and only time since the police raid, but really off.

I know I said before that I was learning to rise above stuff, but maybe you'll think now—or in a moment—that that isn't true. Maybe I'm not the cool, wise daughter of the Goddess that I want to be . . . yet. You decide.

I kicked over a chair—saw it as I was doing it and couldn't believe it—and it went crash up against some kid's desk. The kid who said that last thing in fact. And I said:

'Right! Shut up. Just stoating shut up and listen and

you can find out why I'm stoating well stuck here with you lot, 'cause I certainly wouldn't choose that. Not choose *you* and this miserable place over what I am normally.'

I could see Miss Gibbons closing in near me, wondering if she had a real crisis on her hands, I expect . . . wondering if she should get out the straitjacket or break the fire alarm. So with a huge effort I half turned to her and said:

'Look, I'm sorry. Sorry about the chair. But I *must* say this. Just give me a couple more minutes. Please.' And after looking at me searchingly a moment she drew back slightly and left me to it. Left me telling them about Silver Wind going walking early one morning with her sampling kit and not coming back.

Whether she'd already spotted it and was going out to get the proof, or whether the farmer and his mates just jumped to conclusions, seeing her in the crop like that, Mum must have been caught and taken amongst those still-green wheat stalks. I could visualize it perfectly in my head and knew it was true.

It was Stefan who had enough knowledge to work out *what* it was they'd be testing, secretly like that.

'Wheat!' I told my classmates now. 'Wheat . . . but sterile. You know what that means? Do you? It means that those little golden seeds can get used for our flour *this* year, but are no good for making new plants *next* season. Some idiot has messed about with the plants so that they're sterile and so that farmers all over the world will end up having to come back and buy new seeds every time they want a crop. Oh, yeah, the plants look normal and grow normally; even quicker than normal, which is what'll make the farmers want to buy the stuff in the beginning . . . but . . . '

Oh wow, it made me so sick inside.

Something that some evil joke of a scientist, working for one of those huge American companies, made. Those companies want everything, they want to swallow our beautiful world whole or put a big 'patent' stamp on the bottom of it . . . somewhere round Antarctica maybe. (There could already be one there for all I know!) If you *don't* know about all this yet, then know now! There are guys out there who are playing with the creation of life like it's some computer game . . . and *then* they get to patent, to own, what they make. Which means that some day people will have to pay $x for their baby to have red hair and blue eyes or to be a good athlete, and $y to even plant seeds made by their own crops, because the genes of those people and those crops will be 'owned' by someone. And the Goddess is going to fill the world with her tears because her children are lost and dead, and the gifts She gave will be broken ashes.

And the sickest thing was that *these* children, the ones I was talking to, just didn't care, didn't understand, didn't know a thing. I was half crying and they only thought I was an emotional hippy weirdo. They'd got their show in the end, what they'd turned up for, but it bored and disgusted them.

'Don't you understand?' I said, desperately. 'This is something the government promised wouldn't be done here, but they're doing it anyway, in secret. Kidnapping people to protect themselves. Slipping things in to our lives bit by bit so we have to accept it. And what if this gene crosses by accident into other grains? Into rice and the rest . . . '

Even as I was saying this, the bell was ringing and they were pouring out of there in relief.

'You want to know what it means to be a Traveller? Well, to me it means not messing with the miracle we've been given.'

But I was talking to myself. Like maybe I am right now with you.

It's OK, I understand. Most people *do* think I'm nuts.

Well, after that, after pouring it all out like an idiot, and feeling pretty drained, there was only Miss Gibbons there, and she had her arm round me and was saying:

'It's OK, Kez. Everything's OK. Why not go home now, take the rest of the day off if you like. I'll sort it out with the school office.'

I looked at her and said: 'It's all true, really. That's why I'm here. That's why Mrs Cotterell brought me to London . . .'

Oh wow! It hit me: Brenda Cotterell! Stefan's voice floated into my head, talking about the experimenters: *It's obvious now what they've been doing, Number 99: trying to keep everyone's attention focused away from that farm. Your mum was the expert and they've removed her . . . but anyone else, anyone she might have talked to, anyone who has some connection or might get too nosy, they've all been scattered about the country like your friends and you, or hampered and slowed down, like me. They haven't got much longer, you see? Just four weeks, maybe less, to keep us neutral. Then after the harvest we won't be able to hurt them. So above all we MUST carry on letting them think they've succeeded. The worst thing of all would be to let them know we've worked out their secret. Otherwise, they might do anything . . .*

We could only guess about Mum, follow our instincts, hope she was unharmed. But any chance she had of that was likely to spiral right down to zero if the wheat people got stirred up.

I'd been an idiot. I never learned.

I turned, white-faced, to my teacher. 'Look, miss; Mrs Cotterell really mustn't know what I said today. She *won't* know . . . will she?'

I don't think Miss Gibbons believed my story any more than the others did, but she said kindly, 'Oh no, I don't think she needs to know. Just get some rest, Kez. That's all. We'll see you tomorrow.'

All right. Thank you.

I didn't get any rest.

I didn't see her tomorrow.

When I left the school gates Joe was waiting for me and he was in trouble.

9

He must have been waiting a bit along the street because I found him limping along next to me before I'd got a hundred metres down towards Rose's. He had a bag slung over his shoulder and he was sweating, maybe from running on his dodgy leg. He looked like he needed some looking after. This wasn't the usual cool, quiet Joe: something had got to him. I could feel the panic. My idiocy in the classroom fled from my thoughts.

'I missed you,' I said. 'What's wrong?'

'Here, this way, down here.' He took my elbow and steered me round into a smaller street, one that cut up diagonally from the Camberwell-to-Peckham road on to the big route going up towards the Elephant and Westminster and into the city, missing out the corner with Camberwell Green on it.

'What's up, Joe? Are we trying to miss someone?'

Stupid question.

'*Yes*, we are trying to miss someone. My brother.

Sweet-Talk. Just about everyone, girl. That's who we trying to miss.'

It's lovely to share with friends. Now we could both panic.

'Tell me.'

'Nothing to tell. Nothing. I just been a fool, that's all.' He took a deep breath and shook his head. 'See, Rocket's got a big deal going with Sweet-Talk. Get out of all that trouble with him for ever. Pay the debt. Only *Rocket* been playing the field. He was going to cut Sweet out of the deal, take it all for himself. So . . . I stopped that deal. Stopped my fool brother going down yet.'

I said, trying to make a bit of a joke of it, 'That doesn't sound like nothing, Joe.'

He hurried on without answering.

'How did you stop it? And do they know? . . . That it was you, I mean?'

'Oh yes, girl, they know. They all know. They done lost half a million and Sweet know now that my brother was gonna take it all. Oh, it's *easy* to stop a deal . . .'

He didn't tell me how, which was fine.

By my reckoning, both Rocket and Sweet-Talk were now after Joe. It was a change, I thought, from Brenda and Jag-burning heavies. Someone else's problem, except that he was my friend.

'So what d'you want to do?' I asked.

'I want to get out! *Now*. Out of London. I knew you was thinking of disappearing: you and me could go together. Get back to your people. One place they ain't going to find me is on the road with gypsies!'

Oh, Goddess! The thing I couldn't do right now was disappear. I was supposed to be being a lamb: I'd promised Troll and Stefan. Not rocking the wheat-project boat. Not getting Farmer Spit and his government mates twitchy. Not getting the Jag thugs after me. If Silver Wind was still alive, a prisoner maybe, the best chance was to pretend we didn't know anything about it.

Yeah, except for presentations by one-brain-cell life-forms to their class, of course.

Despite myself I started to giggle. What a mess! And Joe wanting to be a gypsy! It was too much.

'What you laughing at, girl? You think I don't mean this thing? You think they won't kill me as easy as a blink? With thousands lost?'

'No, Joe,' I said between giggles, 'I don't think you're kidding, and I'm not either. I promise. And I'm a Traveller, not a gypsy. But I can't leave right now!'

He already knew more or less why I'd come to London, of course. Now, as we walked up between smothering, grey, tower-block housing on the right and newly-expensive crumbling Victorian terraces on the left, I let him in on the whole lot—the second time that afternoon that I'd let it all pour out, but more controlled this time—and he could see why leaving wasn't a good idea for me.

He rubbed a hand over his lovely tight-curled hair. 'So what'm I gonna do? Can I go on, by myself, meet your friends?'

Um . . . not such a great idea really. Joe was a pure London boy, and black (which means immediately suspect in the eyes of the law) and I could see him getting in all kinds of trouble crossing the country to try and find Troll. Also, just in case, *just in case* Rocket and his thugs could find him somehow, I didn't want to give Troll that big extra headache when he was working on getting Mum back.

But there was one other thing we might try.

'Joe,' I said, 'do you know anyone at the Elephant? Or do *they* know *you*?'

'The Elephant? No, too far north for the gangs round here. They'll have connections maybe, but . . . '

'OK then, how d'you fancy selling old hippy clothes for a week or two? We can disguise you, you know, with sunglasses, Hendrix hat . . . all sorts of stuff!'

The thing was, though (like Stefan) he'd told me to stay put, Troll was worried about me. Sweet. So Ron had volunteered to pull himself away from festivals and get back to the old pitch, just to be able to help if help was needed, only a call away. He'd also be our link with Troll. He was supposed to be back there, van and all, from Wednesday—which was tomorrow. Hannah was going to keep half the stock and Jake would help her with that as he carried on trying to gather up all the others through the festival network.

I could just see sweet, serious Joe in purple silk scarf, sheepskin waistcoat, and flares.

Well, what else was there? If he hung around near me or at Rose's, we'd all end up getting hurt. I didn't reckon that any of the last ninety-eight kids had put Rose in the middle of so much weird and dangerous stuff. I certainly didn't want to make it any worse.

Joe wasn't exactly over the moon about the stall idea, but he got a lot more into it about two minutes later, just as we were reaching the main road. Behind us and quite distinctive even with the endless background rumble of London traffic, there came the growl of a powerful engine that had had someone monkeying about with the exhaust to make it sound even more charged up. Also it was being driven fast, too fast for in-town.

I'd only heard it once before but I was pretty sure it was Rocket's BMW. Joe recognized it at the same moment and yelled, 'Go, girl!', but I was already grabbing his rucksack and his arm and diving for the main road. Maybe, just maybe, we'd be safe in all the hubbub.

But maybe not.

For the first time in its history probably, that big route up into town had no convenient old-fashioned buses to jump on in the grinding lines of traffic, and hardly any people around down the pavements next to the curry houses and video places. Behind us, the car was coming right up. They'd seen us now and started leaning on the horn for us to stop. Help! If we ran up towards the city, well, true they'd have to turn *across* the traffic and into the queues, but that way the shops and everything ended for a while and it turned back into sixties flat blocks, typical gang territory. So we went left instead, giving them an easy turn, but crossing over quickly through the cars so they couldn't actually come up on the pavement and drive straight at us. If we were lucky a bus might appear in time—Joe was starting to stumble on his bad leg—and if we weren't lucky, Denise's flower place wasn't far down.

It wasn't exactly fair to bring the nasties to meet cheerful, birdlike Denise, but I didn't think I'd ever see Joe again if they got him into their car. Maybe we could phone from the shop or something. Since it wasn't about Silver Wind this time maybe the stoating law would even help us for once, scream out to the sodding rescue. ('Yeah right,' the kids in my class would say.)

Well, we made it; but not by much. When we crashed into the shop doorway Joe had already gone down once and had blood on his forearms, and my breathing in that stinking chemical air felt like someone was kneeling on my chest. Seeing we were fading, the thugs had parked up at an angle on the opposite pavement and were crossing unhurriedly after us on foot, gold jewellery rattling away under red leather coats. There were only two, Rocket and another one, but two was more than enough in the shape we were in.

No doubt the little boys had brought their little guns to play with too.

I banged the shop door open with my shoulder and pushed Joe inside amongst the stacked buckets of flowers, yelling, 'Denise! De*nise*! Help Joe: get him out! I'm sorry, Denise! Nowhere else . . . '

That was about all there was time for. Rocket and friend were right there on the pavement, showing their teeth at the easy kill, walking in the silly way they thought big men with guns should walk. I shut the door behind me and stood in their way. After all, it wasn't me they wanted, and maybe Denise could get Joe out the back and away, or phone or something. Yeah, pretty thick of me, I know, but I think I was just so desperate to *do* something after not hitting back at anyone for so long. Goddess, they weren't exactly going to shoot some thirteen-year-old girl in the middle of the street in daytime . . . were they?

The grins got bigger.

'Hey, the little piece of trash is pro-*tect*-ing the cripple,' Rocket said. 'What she think she gonna do, give us her disease?'

I *really* didn't like Rocket.

He lazily reached out to move me out the way like fluff off his shoulder and I swung Joe's bag up on to his chin (*something* nice and solid was in that bag!) and then kicked him in the place where girls are supposed to kick drug-dealing thugs as a last resort.

'Argghhh, *bitch*!' he screamed hopping about clutching himself. If he hadn't needed both hands to massage his damaged pride he probably *would* have got his gun out and shot me after all. As it was, he didn't need to because his friend, less worried about being cool, flicked his hand through the air and *bang* into my temple, one of his chunky rings ploughing into the skin for extra fun. And that was me down, on the pavement with the litter and the dirt and not quite focusing. So much for wanting to do something.

Blearily, I saw thug number two wrench open the flower shop door and then stop in surprise as Denise bounced cheerfully out, minus Joe, like she had a customer who wanted a mixed bouquet for twenty quid. The thug was shouting something at her. Not something repeatable. Denise shrugged happily and now the thug was patting his jacket and getting even angrier. I couldn't see what she was doing. Maybe trying to get other people to notice? There were a few other shopkeepers and shoppers around now, watching from a safe distance, of course. Rocket had staggered back to life and he joined his friend, shouting too, except *he* actually had his hand inside his coat. *Please*, I thought, *don't let Denise be shot because of me*.

After some more shouting she'd done it: there were *a lot* of people starting to gather now. Mostly still some distance away, but witnesses anyway.

But I saw at the same time that it was no good. Rocket didn't care. People wired up on coke or speed *don't* care, do they? Maybe it was even my fault for kicking him like that, driving him over the edge. I saw him take out a heavy, black gun and heard someone—me—sob 'No!', and then . . .

. . . then some incredible miracle happened.

Through the blood coming into my eye I saw the small, slight Denise in her grubby flower shop shirt and torn jeans neatly kick the gun from Rocket's hand and with the same movement stamp firmly down on his knee. *Crunch*, Rocket was down. Then she was back in some sort of low crouching pose, facing the second nasty. *He*—definitely minus all cool by this time and looking a jerk—thought about his choices, looked around at his growing audience, and then hauled the screaming Rocket to his feet and bodily dragged him back over the road, through the traffic and to the BMW. No silly walk.

There was quite a lot of clapping as the scarlet car

screeched off and suddenly all the people that hadn't quite wanted to be there before were offering help and advice and making jokes about Denise being too tough to sell flowers.

It was a relief when she pushed them all away, shut the blinds, locked the door of the shop and took me into the back where Joe was calmly drinking tea. I went and sat on his lap and helped myself to his tea. I thought he owed me that, at least.

Black belt or not, Denise decided that she'd clear out of the shop and the bedsit above it for a few days.

Joe agreed.

'Oh yeah,' he said, grinning, 'they come back again soon. Losers like my brother got this thing about being beat. An' being beat by a girl will give him hell with those other losers. *An'* he still want me.'

Up the girls' team, I thought silently, and for the little boys let the Goddess strip them down to their nothingness so they just blow away in the wind.

That day ended by Stefan—bemused as ever—having to give his newly-rented floor space to both Joe and Denise. I went home to Rose because I had to really, for any wheat watchers. The next day, though, I risked Brenda Cotterell coming to school to moan about me again by skipping off and getting the bus up to the Elephant to fix Joe up with Ron the Pirate. I was very careful to switch buses and stuff a few times in case I *was* actually being watched all the time now and also because of Joe's brother, although Denise said very matter-of-factly that she'd broken his knee and he wouldn't be around for a while.

I was thinking about that, about Rocket maybe ending up with a bad leg like Joe—and wondering if it was some kind of balance—when the Number 12 went past the flower shop, past great wedges of broken glass and scattered stems and flower buckets and rude words sprayed over everything.

Poor Denise! I seemed at the moment to be someone it was better not to know.

She took it OK, said it was all insured and that the law might even get some witnesses. For the moment, she and Joe and Stefan carried on rooming together, with Stefan gloomily making a show of starting his new study into pedestrian crossings (rattling off in his rustbucket XR2), Joe shiftily wearing shades and felt hat behind the clothes stall and Denise hiring a tiny van to carry on doing her flowers at markets until the shop was sorted out by the insurance people.

I told Rose enough about what had happened for her not to worry too much about Denise ('Oh yes, dear, she's been doing that *karate* since . . . you know . . . since the trouble with her father. Did her own club in the evenings for a while.') and went back to school life, endless boring hours of algebra and Religious Studies and getting called everything under the sun by unhappy, trapped dimwits staring at their toes.

After the whole deal with my presentation, exposing myself like that too, I was itching to be out of there and leave the little Camberwell bubble to its own thoughts again. Somewhere in a police pound the old Bedford was waiting, wanting to be filled with human brightness like before. I felt guilty about Rose—wanting to leave her house that is, after she was so amazingly good to me—but she didn't blame me. There was stuff we all wanted to get sorted out and over with and until then it was a twitchy kind of limbo.

Troll reckoned that if Mum was a prisoner she'd actually be in Rook Rise itself. Logical to keep the illegal stuff all in one place, he said, but just a guess. Let's face it, *everything* was just a guess, even the thing about the GM wheat. Stefan was out of his depth, too. *He* didn't think anyone from the government would want people hurt, but then they might have teamed up with a nastier bunch who saw things differently. Whatever the truth was, the safest thing seemed to be that we stayed hyper-careful until Troll managed to find out anything new, some proof of where Mum was, perhaps. If that happened we were to get a signal through Ron.

For the moment we had to pretend to know nothing, and imagine being watched and listened to all the time.

So the dust-filled heat got worse, tempers were short and I kept a bag packed ready for Troll's call.

Rose said one day, 'Is it my imagination, dear, or is Mrs Cotterell calling more often again now? She's giving me the pip, breathing down our necks like this.'

Three weeks until harvest we reckoned, then getting close to only two! I started to fret that Troll and Stefan were wrong after all, about Silver Wind. They both thought that *if* she was still unharmed—and hidden at Rook Rise farm—then she'd stay safe at least until the moment of harvest as nobody would want bodies turning up to draw attention to them. *Our* aim was to have a plan ready so that we could get her back at that exact moment when they'd all be concentrating on something else.

Pretty lame, I started to think. Or even just plain nuts. Ringed by doubts and guesses, I prayed hard to the Goddess.

After school, with no Joe or anyone much to see, I started walking aimlessly round the streets, jumping on buses to see where they went, or sitting on the Green watching the tortured snakes of traffic.

I wanted more than anything to be next to some clear cold river where I could just strip off and dive to the bottom. The water would be a freezing, breathless shock, cleaning me and raising goosebumps on my arms. Yummy. I needed something like that to get the London grime out of me.

When things finally did start to move—and they moved very fast!—it was while I was doing that, lolling about on some bench at the Green late one afternoon, dreaming of an icy rebirth.

10

'Mrs Payne? Hello? Mrs Payne? Rose?'

The door was open, which wasn't right, and no sounds, none of Rose's usual clatter as she got supper. Only the hum and roar from the main road I'd just left. When I found her, sitting at the kitchen table, I thought it was all OK—that she was just sitting having a think or something . . . but then she turned towards me and the evening light caught her face. It was all puffed up on one side. When she spoke her voice was a bit funny, indistinct and lost.

'Sorry, Kez,' she said quietly, 'I wasn't expecting it, you see. They just barged in when I opened the door. The chain didn't stop them at all.'

'Who was it, Mrs Payne? *Who* barged in? Was it the wheat people?' I filled the kettle to make some tea and wondered if she had any whisky or something to put in it. I was so angry with myself. If only I'd come back straight after school instead of hanging about like a moron!

'Not them. Some others; after your friend Joe. They

asked where he was. I said I didn't know. They left a number. There, on that paper. We're to ring them and tell them about Joe or they'll . . . come back.'

I gave her the tea, topped up with some Co-op brandy that was in with the spices and flour, probably left from Christmas. She wouldn't let me call a doctor or the police, just sat sipping her drink, so it was obvious what I had to do next. There was no way that Rose could get hurt, not for me or for anyone else. I dialled the number the big *men* had left and told them that Joe would be at the stall in the Elephant the next morning. That gave us a bit of time to get sorted out and I went out and got some food for the two of us, pizza and salad from a place up the street.

When we'd eaten and Rose was getting back to normal and parked next to her radio, I used the phone again and got Joe on Stefan's mobile.

'You understand? They've gotta see you there in the morning or they'll think I lied and come back for Rose. You and Ron have got to sort something out: some plan where they see you like you didn't expect it and weren't warned, but you still get away. Yeah, I know it doesn't sound exactly easy . . . but Rose's got to come first.'

Joe saw that and there was no blame or anything.

'Sure, girl, we can do that . . . have to think how, though . . . and where I can go after that.'

I think he wanted a suggestion from me. Too bad, I just didn't have one. This was his city, not mine. After all, with so little time now till the early harvest at Rook Rise Farm he should get by OK, even if he just stayed locked in Stefan's place.

I didn't *say* that, of course, in case we were being listened to, but then I was just asking if Joe could sing— to go busking somewhere in the city—when I realized that *he* didn't know about the phone. I hadn't told him about possible bugs. And at that moment, suddenly suspended in time, I *knew* he was going to blow it, right then, in the next thing he said. Don't ask me how. I made my voice louder and carried on speaking, anything that came into my head, just to not give him a space.

At the same time the listening part of my brain heard him say, quite clearly, 'D'you reckon your friends will find some way of sorting them wheat people soon, so we can split from here?'

'*JOE!*' I screamed it, but it was too late.

There was a pause and I was thinking like crazy, what we had to do.

'Babe?' Joe sounded confused. 'What's up, Kez? What is it, girl?'

Keep calm, I thought, *be cool. Think!*

'OK . . . OK, Joe, listen, is Stefan still there?'

'Yeah, in the bath.'

'OK, good. You go and tell him then what you just said to me. Tell him all we said in this call, OK? (*Think, Kez, don't give anything else away, just in case.*) Tell him . . . tell him I'll be where your brother first saw us together—when you kissed me—I'll be there in half an hour and wait for you both until you come.'

Then I just put the phone down, in case dear Joe hadn't got it yet and wanted to say more.

My hands were shaking as I stuffed my toothbrush in the ready-packed bag and took a last look at the gloomy little room that had been home for a few weeks. Now it came to it I knew it had been a blessing—that Rose had been a blessing. Her Number 99 was fighting tears when it came to the hurried goodbye, leaving her all bruised and alone, even though she understood.

'You go, dear! Go and find your mother and bring her back to see me one day. And . . . you and Stefan keep each other safe! You're a survivor, Kez, and even he is, in his own way.'

I started to reply, but she pushed me into the hall and along to the door.

'Hurry now, dear. I'll be fine. But you go now, just in case someone does come!'

Then I was out into the warm night, jogging softly down on to the Peckham road, checking back over my shoulder for buses, and despite myself feeling not only the worry and sadness of leaving Rose like that, but also a growing excitement. A sheer stoating joy at being on the move again . . . at breaking free and *moving* at last.

Nobody would kill Silver Wind, I told myself, not just because of that call, not at least until harvest and they were safe, not without knowing what *we* had on them. It was *us* who were in most danger from any phone listeners. If Mum was OK now then she'd stay OK. Nothing had really changed . . .

I didn't know if I believed that or not. Joe's mistake had set it all moving and there was nothing I could do but move with it. Abandoning the idea of a bus I ran headlong, bursting with release, through the London night.

It was midnight near enough by the time they came and by then the excitement had taken a bit of a battering. Well, you try hanging about Peckham Rye in the middle of the night and you'll see why. Still, they *did* show up, the Fiesta chugging to a halt, all crammed with stuff that they must've thought we'd need.

Some people aren't so good at travelling light. Giggle. Stefan even had a neatly pressed suit hanging up in the back.

Both Joe and Stefan were pretty wired up too, I could feel it.

'In you hop then, 99,' Stefan said, quite cheerfully,

and Joe slid into the back, leaning forward to say in my ear 'Sorry . . . I blew it, I know,' though he had probably the most reason to be glad we were moving. His hand snaked round the side of the seat as we started off and I held it with mine and squeezed it to say it was all OK, cool about his mistake.

Where we were going next and what we were going to do, now we were officially fugitives from the wheat nasties, wasn't that easy to decide, though. Joe was into leaving London behind as soon as we could, but for Rose's sake and safety *he* had to be on display at the stall tomorrow morning, at least until Rocket's or Sweet-Talk's people turned up. Also, if the enemy *had* listened in to us then perhaps just charging down to Basingstoke wasn't too clever. We still had no idea if Troll had worked out a plan or got more info or anything and we could easily just end up putting Silver Wind in more danger than before . . . or getting ourselves beaten up or worse.

Stefan agreed. 'We need to drop out of sight for a while, not tread on anyone's toes until things cool off, leave them guessing a bit too. I propose that we stay in a hotel tonight under false names, my treat, and have a think. The first little thing anyway is to work out how we're going to play the scene where our friend Joe escapes by the skin of his teeth in the morning, without appearing to have been warned.'

He talked on as he drove, going over the cloak-and-dagger stuff he thought we'd have to learn—and I reckon he was starting to enjoy it like boys do with things like that. He said that the people we were up against would be good, very good. We'd need to ditch the Fiesta or hide it when we could, all payments for things like hotels would have to be cash to avoid cards being traced . . .

Then he said he thought I should get my lovely hair cut off.

'NO! No stoating way!' I said. There were limits.

'Come on, 99,' he said, laughing at me. 'You're so easy to spot like that, so easy to describe to hotel staff or anybody. I tell you what: we'll book you in for a lovely session in some cosy salon tomorrow and then I'll buy you a new dress.'

I didn't wear dresses: hadn't he noticed? And what about his poncy suits? Was he going to ditch them? Oh, sure!

All this time we were motoring back into town, then over the river (we went over Tower Bridge this time, just in case) and up towards the north of the city. When Stefan stopped at a cashpoint for hotel money his good mood got pole-axed and I was almost (*almost*, but not really) pleased after his plans for my dreads.

'Damned thing swallowed my card! They must have already stopped my account . . . '

He broke off and we sat in silence in that car, all realizing what he'd just said.

Unless there was some horrible, weird coincidence happening, this was proof. *They* knew about us. *They* had been watching. And their reach was long, powerful, frightening.

Stefan angrily accelerated off from the kerb and we still said nothing. In shock, I suppose. On the good side, I thought numbly, hotels and fancy haircuts and dresses were not going to happen now: we were back in the real world!

We kept on driving and eventually parked up at the end of a tiny cul-de-sac that we found, in a place called Stoke Newington. Most of the buildings in the cul-de-sac were lock-up garages and stuff. Stefan wearily voiced our thoughts: 'Well, at least we know for certain that they *are* on to us. We might as well try and get a few hours rest. I've got about thirty pounds on me and that's it. Anyone else got anything?'

Joe had twelve pounds and I had three. Not really a fortune, but I wasn't too troubled. This was *my* lifestyle and there were ways to get by. Already I was starting to have an idea, one that I thought I'd leave till the morning. Despite everything I found that I was really still quite cheerful. The only bad thing was having to crash out in a Fiesta overnight. If you've never slept in a Fiesta with two other people, then—like hanging about at night on Peckham Rye—it's something that can't really be described! Try it.

Ron the Pirate had his stall up and most of the stuff already spread out when we motored back down over the river to the Elephant, even though it was only seven. Like us, he'd slept parked up somewhere in his vehicle, but with him it was a Transit filled with nice soft boxes of cotton, velvet, and silk, a perfect place to spread out. Stefan winced and rubbed his neck and looked jealous. A tuft of flattened hair stuck up funnily over one ear like a single horn and unusual stubble was growing through. Joe had done better, spread out diagonally in the back of the car; and I'd got up early and done some stretching and yoga—a favourite ritual thing of mine where you welcome the new sun—so I felt light-headed and calm.

'Yeah . . . wow . . . got you . . . cool thought . . . '

Ron nodded seriously. We were sitting in the Transit cab while he listened to the tale of last night's excitement. I could see that he was pleased that now he'd be able to get back down to Hannah and away from London, and he was already two steps ahead of my next thought.

'So you'd like me to try and see Troll, maybe, and tell him what's going down. I can't phone him, you know. But I could send him up to find you? Or arrange a meeting.'

'Yes please.'

'No sweat.' He gave a pirate's grin. 'You could come too.'

I'd already thought of that of course and wanted it very much, but there were things against it. The wheat people knew about Troll and would be looking for him themselves, probably much harder than before now, maybe even sending people into the festivals and all that. So better to have two teams for them to look for . . . and two to try and get Silver Wind back if it came to that.

And also I felt that I owed something to Stefan and Joe, almost like I should look after them now we were on the road, sort of.

'So what about these guys coming for Joe-boy? What do we do with them?' Ron sounded like he was pointing out the weather or something, not at all hassled by the idea of the visit.

'Well . . . all we could think of was that Joe should run down the tube steps: he should be able to get there in a few seconds and if it's crowded his leg won't slow him down much more than the others. Then Stefan and me will try and slow them down somehow, to give him more start . . . and we'll pick Joe up again at some other station.'

It was only maybe fifty metres to the tube station but telling Ron the plan I could see how weak it sounded.

Ron saw it too.

'Yeah . . . well . . . aren't they supposed not to see you, so they don't think he was warned off? Be pretty obvious he was waiting if you and Stefan start knocking them down, tripping them up, whatever. And what if he doesn't make it on that leg, man?'

I didn't answer. He gazed sightlessly out of the windscreen from his castle in the clouds.

'Maybe we can make it work . . . maybe . . . '

Outside the van Joe was already doing business on the

stall, charming the customers, flashing his teeth, and selling like he was born to it, trusting the rest of us to take care of the escape details. Stefan came in sight round the corner carrying polystyrene cups of tea so I let myself gently out of the cab and left Ron to his thoughts.

'What did he think?'

'Not much. He's working on it.'

Joe said with a half-smile, 'Sweet-Talk's people don't wake early most days . . . but maybe we should have something set up soon, you know? Not that I don't have faith in the man, babe . . . '

'Relax,' I said. The big open space that was the Elephant was starting to fill up with cars and people. Every time a tube arrived under our feet there was another deluge of crushed bodies out on to the pavements. Buses were stopping and starting in rows along the length of the kerb (voted against for Joe's getaway because they were so easy to follow) and taxis and minicabs swooped up against any spare bits of pavement and took off again. I didn't think there was much chance we'd spot the nasties when they did come, although they might be watching *us* even now.

Ron opened the door of the van, letting out a cloud of tangy smoke.

'OK, guys,' he said, 'this is what we're gonna do . . . '

11

When they did appear it was suddenly and without warning, like I'd thought.

I don't know if Joe knew them at all, but they were new faces to me, two guys walking along the pavement in opposite directions, one looking at a trashy paper, the other smoking, not seeming to know each other or anything. Only one was black and for some reason I'd been silly enough to be looking out just for black guys. Good thing Stefan and I were well out of it, at least two hundred metres away at some samosa-and-doughnut place just in case back-up was needed, 'cause I probably would have blown it by now.

It was only when these two guys drew level with the stall from their opposite directions that they came suddenly alive in the worst way, one without warning already behind the stall gripping Joe's arm and the second on the other side, blocking any possible escape. Ron was stuck in the middle with Joe. They weren't interested in him, of course, but after the thing with Denise they'd probably been told to be careful, so as soon as he started to make a fuss, getting Joe's other arm and trying to push the thug away, man number two moved in and brought something down on the back of his head.

Another in the growing line of casualties that had only one thing in common between them . . . knowing me. Poor Ron.

Hearing some kind of trouble, the guy with the next stall along—the sunglasses—poked his head round to see if Ron was OK. 'It'll all look very innocent, cool, unplanned;' Ron had said. 'The other stall folk will gradually move in and get involved, hamper your villains, make any real violence impossible. Just loyal market people looking out for their own. Somehow Joe's got to slip away when it's all getting going.' And that's exactly how it worked. Sunglasses, who was round and bald and amiable looking, was there asking Ron if he was OK, asking what was going on, calling out to his mate further down the line to come and have a look. Then the fruit lady, wrinkled and hard as nails, heard the fuss and came too to see. One by one, stallholders left their pitches and gathered round the clothes stall, helping Ron back to his feet, asking what the nasties were up to, why they were holding that boy.

We couldn't hear anything that was said, of course, from where we were, but the whole thing was like a beautiful ballet, and the thugs gradually lost their purpose, got swamped by too many people ready to stick up for a fellow trader . . . and finally let go of Joe for an instant.

That's when I saw thug number three.

As soon as Joe was away, putting distance between himself and the first two, crowded-in attackers, another guy was after him. He must have been watching as back-up, from over the road, and right now he was haring across, weaving through the traffic to try and cut Joe off at the tube station. Another face that I didn't know and hopefully didn't know me and this time there was no choice anyway.

'Stefan! They're gonna get him! There's another one!' I was already running along the pavement towards the unsuspecting Joe, who'd himself almost got to the tube entrance but just *wasn't* going to make it. I could hear Stefan following me, breathing hard. At the same time I could see that the first two nasties, further along the street, had managed finally to break free of the knot of traders and were hurrying to join the fun. If there hadn't been that third one then Ron's plan would have been perfect, slowing them down just enough.

Then, as I was maybe twenty metres from Joe and he was about to be grabbed, I saw, slow-motion style, two *more* guys moving in on the station entrance . . . but these were *much* bigger—much wider and more menacing and calmer—than the others, and they weren't looking at Joe, they were looking at me. I had a chilling thought and stopped to share it with Stefan, but when I turned half round I saw that he had two more of the wide ones behind him.

Was there any stoating person at the Elephant that morning *not* trying to get us for some reason, I thought?

The bit of pavement we were on now had those solid metal railings on one side to keep people from falling into the busy traffic and unless we hopped over we were both going to be bottled in. There was just a chance that we could make the tube steps before the ones ahead, but no way that they'd let us queue for rush-hour tickets before taking up the chase.

'Wheat people . . . ' I gasped back over my shoulder, ' . . . jump the barriers!'

Stefan said something back but I didn't catch it. I just went flat out those last few metres, thankful that being built like houses made thugs a bit cocky and a bit slow. As I spun into the tiled entrance I saw that Joe had been grabbed but had managed to push his guy down. He was looking round wildly because, trying to be too clever, we'd paid some local kid a fiver to just be standing waiting to hand a ticket to the escaping Joe and the little runt hadn't bothered to keep his side of the bargain. Joe's moment of panic and not being sure what to do meant that the guy on the floor was getting up again and the first two were already coming right in behind us, alongside a breathless Stefan and then followed by the four that were after me rather than Joe.

What a mess.

Stefan and I *might* still make the barriers, but Joe didn't look like he would.

OK, I thought, let's increase the panic . . . and yelled *'Police!'* at the top of my voice.

Yelling that in most bits of South London will probably have some sort of effect and this time it was pure magic. The three guys sent by Sweet-Talk stopped short, swung round and saw the four slowly advancing bouncers and assumed from long habit that *they* were the target. All thought of Joe went out of them and instead they spun round and made to get back out the entrance. One had a gun out and fired a shot upwards to clear the way and warn what he probably thought were unarmed CID that they should move too. It certainly got their attention. One of the wide-shouldered boys casually stuck out his arm and knocked down a running gang member, keeping him squirming on the floor with his foot. The other two were out, but one of the wheat thugs was reaching inside his jacket and jogging after them and I thought I fancied his chances if he got hold of them.

The other two were undeflected, worse luck, still homed-in on us like terriers . . .

And that was as much as I could see or wanted to see. I had Joe's hand and we were up and over the stainless steel barriers, with Stefan right there next to us. Then a clattering, headlong rush down endless spiral stairs—it's one of those stations with a lift if you're not in a hurry—and on to the first train we could grab.

The whole thing from leaving the samosa stall to getting on the train took maybe two minutes and felt like ten.

Of course the spot fines for fare-dodging when we got out, two stations up, more or less cleaned us out of any remaining money, but we were all shivering and high on adrenalin and frightened half to hell so it didn't really seem a big deal, in return for having made it in one piece.

'Two of those were definitely the ones I saw when I got bumped on the head before. We might as well assume,' Stefan said gloomily, 'that they know what car I'm driving now and may even have already picked it up. Also, that they got at least one of those people chasing Joe and probably Ron too. Also that they know all my friends and acquaintances and anywhere that I might go to borrow more money. Which means that they know everything useful there is to know about all three of us and that we have no money. If I were them I'd be quite optimistic of a result. Any ideas, anyone?'

We'd cooled off and calmed down now and were sat in a café, spending our last few pounds on something to eat and drink, keeping off the streets for an hour or two, just in case. Both Stefan and Joe were totally down, but again I couldn't help feeling the excitement of being left with nothing . . . the way we are born. Totally free to make our way, if only we could think clearly enough. I hoped with all my heart that he was wrong about Ron, though, after all the help we'd had. And also because Ron was the one link we had with Troll.

Troll would have left Glastonbury. He was probably back near Basingstoke or Rook Rise, watching for evidence of Mum, making plans; but we couldn't be sure.

I said, 'The first thing is probably to lose my dreads like you said, and maybe see what else we can do to change how we look.'

'But you were all against that before!'

'Yeah, changed my mind. You were right, Number 1.'

Joe said, 'Where are haircuts gonna come from, with no bread? And food.'

'There are ways!' I pinched the tip of his nose with my thumb and finger, like you do with a child, and tried to look as mysterious as possible to tease him. 'All things are possible. The trouble with you and Stefan is you're not used to life on the road.'

Stefan gave me a funny look over his cup rim. 'Er . . . excuse me. I don't suppose then that Rose ever told you? Where I come from, originally?'

'No: she said I should ask you myself, "one waif and stray to another". But we haven't exactly had time . . . '

Stefan pinched the end of *my* nose.

'Dear Kez . . . my parents were Romanies in Czechoslovakia. I spent the first years of my life in a caravan. I was smuggled out when the Russians invaded in 1968, sent with a friend and supposed to meet my parents again here in England.' He paused. 'Then they didn't make it. So I was placed with Rose and John. Their first foster child.'

I couldn't believe it. It was so perfect and sort of balanced that Stefan should turn out to be a Traveller too. Rose's first kid and her last one both born on the road.

I said, 'OK. So here we are: a real live gypsy, a New

Age Traveller, and a wannabe Traveller with all his bridges burnt. We just can't go wrong.'

Somehow I didn't get the feeling that they agreed, but as they had no other ideas they walked with me to Covent Garden, where I said we could get some money.

'So now what?' Joe asked when we got there. We were right in the centre where Stefan said the old market used to be.

'Now *I'm* going to get my hair cut and you two are going to get some cash!'

'Sweet girl. How we gonna do that? I'm *not* gonna thieve for it, so don't ask.'

'Don't worry,' I smiled, enjoying this bit, knowing what their reaction would be. 'No stealing, thieving, burglary, pickpocketing, or anything. You just have to sing. You two find some nice crowded corner, put a jacket or something on the ground for the money, and then sing some songs to all these tourists and rich people with their suits. You can't miss, even if it's awful, because *someone* will feel sorry for you and throw you a coin! Stefan will remember . . . he's a gypsy!'

I left them complaining and saying 'no way' and all that and went to find the cosy salon like Stefan had suggested before. Three hours sweeping up hair and cleaning and bagging up some old junk, bottles of smelly chemicals and all that, that'd been growing in their cellar probably for years . . . and then they happily gave me a haircut in return, the full treatment. I felt a pang for the dreads, which had been almost down to my bum, but . . . change can be good too.

When I got back to find the singers they were *not* singing, just standing looking around for me like lemons and miserable enough anyway to frighten off anybody that wanted to give them any money. Most of the crowds of tourists and shoppers had gone by now and the shops were shut but I still got about ten metres away from them before they realized who I was.

'Wow!'

They stood gawping at me and I felt myself blushing.

'Oh stoat! It's still *me*, you know. Kez. Number 99. Don't think I'm going to stoating stay like this when we've got Mum back!'

They still looked like frozen goldfish. I began to wish I'd left my hair alone.

'All right! That's it! Show over! How much money did you get?'

The fish turned to sheep. It turned out that Stefan couldn't sing at all—people had just laughed—and Joe had only managed one song by himself before he'd dried up. They'd made one pound eighty.

Oh well. Starvation is supposed to be quite a good spiritual thing, purifying you and all that.

There was one good thing, which was that instead of singing Stefan had been thinking of who he could ask for help and had come up with some woman called Katrina, who he used to go out with but hadn't seen for a long time. He reckoned that the wheat people *might* not know about her. She lived in roughly the right direction for us, just outside Maidenhead, and was rich, beautiful, and apparently still living with her parents in some great big house on the river.

'Why did she go for you then, with all that money and looks and everything? And you must be *much* older. Not surprised she dumped you!'

I was just teasing, but Stefan looked a bit hurt.

'If you must know, *I* . . . "dumped" . . . *her*. We were engaged for a while a few years ago. I can't say what she saw in *me*, but in the beginning I found her attractive, charming, lots of bright young friends, you know, we had a few dates . . . and then I suddenly ended up expected to marry her by her parents. I can't remember ever *deciding* to marry her, or even *asking* to marry her: it was just assumed. Then one morning I woke up and realized I didn't like her one bit. The whole thing turned a bit bloody after that, which is why I shouldn't think anyone's watching her place, even if they know of her existence.'

Joe said, practically, 'An' she won't mind seeing you again?'

'Hmm, not sure. But I shouldn't think she'd actually turn me in to our pursuers or anything.' He looked a bit shifty. 'She *is* a little . . . er . . . snobbish, shall we say. We'd have to be on our best behaviour.'

Oh yes! I was getting a pretty clear picture of Katrina in my mind and reckoned that she was probably racist as well as snobby—the two things often seem to get stuck together—so she'd hardly want to see either me or Joe. Stefan alone, I reckoned, when and if we got there. For now, though, we were stuck in London for a while. The only way out with no money was hitching and that'd be crazy, the three of us stood on a motorway sliproad with some sign: almost asking to get caught. Walking would be OK for me, going slowly cross-country and out of the way, but there was Joe's leg and also we'd need at least some food for that, which brought us back to money.

It was a lovely evening again, for London that is. The sun was still warm on the paving slabs. A lone clown was just setting up on one side of the open market area to get the evening pub trade, red mouth painted downwards for unhappy even though he was whistling away to himself while he spread out his kit. If the boys had managed to make any money we could have just sat down and enjoyed his act with a roll or something, but now Joe and Stefan were just about to do an evening's washing up—or toilet-cleaning, or whatever we could find in the restaurants and pubs around—to get some food or some money. I put on what I hoped was a sweet smile to tell them the good news. Otherwise they'd still be standing there like lost lemons when morning came . . .

After my stint in the hairdresser's cellar I thought *I* deserved something more fun. When I'd sent the other two off I'd see if I could charm the unhappy clown.

We were three more days in London in the end and got quite a good routine going, as far as you can, sleeping rough in a city. Our nights were in Hyde Park, hidden under some prickly bushes and thankful that it was summer. In the morning we paid 50p each to use the toilets in Marble Arch tube station, where we could get cleaned up and all that. Then it was a walk back down the swarming length of Oxford Street and on to Covent Garden, which seemed (from the little I knew) about the best pitch around. With a bit of help Stefan found casual work in a burger place and part of the deal was that the three of us got to sit in the back and eat something twice a day. I got pretty fed up with their veggie beanburger but it was fun seeing Civil Service, E-type Stefan in his red and white washer-up uniform. He had a little badge with his name, even though he wasn't serving anyone.

Joe and I spent the days working the crowds together and got to know each other a lot better, which was lovely. He actually had a sweet voice, quite low and gravelly against my higher one. I taught him some good busking songs we could do together, although he wasn't so quick with the juggling that I also hoped he'd learn to improve our act. (I'd juggled and collected money for the clown that first night and got paid with some juggling stuff to use myself.) Whatever, we did OK, started putting away quite a few fivers to keep us when we left the city . . . and quickly left the pitch and headed into the crowds when the law came too near. Whatever silly thing they might pick us up for would probably have the muscle-men from before homing in again pretty quickly.

Meanwhile I could see a new Joe coming out, more up-for-it and fun and relaxed. He must've had a really horrible time before, back with his nightmare family. He was good at the busking too, like he had been with selling off the stall—natural at charming the crowds, though he was really careful not to let the people listening see that he had a bad leg in case they wanted to give money out of pity. Some people I've met would have used that like crazy! What we did was to have him sing a song on his own every so often while I worked round any audience juggling and collecting money.

With my new haircut I was at least as shy as him I think. I hadn't realized how much I'd used the Traveller image to hide away.

Funny . . . even Stefan with his hands white and wrinkly from endless soap suds and deprived of his suits and car and everything seemed to get more chilled out. Getting rid of *stuff* and routines and just living day-to-day does that to people. I've seen it before. When we reached the target we'd set of a hundred quid earned plus a few bits and pieces from charity shops, extra clothes, a water bottle and things, we were quite a happy threesome on the run. We decided to get the tube out to Heathrow, because anybody watching ways out of London probably wouldn't think of the tube, and then to walk from there to Maidenhead, or get a bus if we saw one on the way or if Joe's leg gave way.

That fourth morning, riding underground out of London back towards my real life, I counted up and reckoned that it was less than a fortnight until the Rook Rise harvest.

I'd been a foster child in the city for more than seven weeks. Bye-bye, Brenda. Grin.

12

At Heathrow, with the agreement of Stefan and Joe, I used a payphone to try Ron's mobile.

Maybe he hadn't been spotted or taken at the Elephant. Maybe he would have made contact with Troll again.

A voice that was completely new to me answered on the fourth ring.

'Listen very carefully,' it said, not even asking for my name. 'The woman Rachel Harrison remains unharmed. I guarantee this. She will continue to be so *only* if there is no interference in our activities. In a period of not less than two weeks, she will be released, still unharmed. The exact timing and location of this release are not important at present. You need only know that this again depends on you. *Any* attempt to interfere in our activities—*or* to involve other agencies, such as the press or the police force—will result in different plans for Rachel Harrison. In such a case I could no longer give you that guarantee of her safety.'

That was it.

Game over.

13

With nowhere much else to go, we went on to Katrina's place anyway.

I don't remember getting there. The powerful waves of feeling inside me, soaring, sobbing relief and terrible, stone-cold fear, made me pretty unaware of anything for a while. The others left me to myself, or maybe they spoke and I didn't notice. I only started to resurface when we got there and were stood in the bushes at the bottom of the drive.

'Hey, this ain't my league at *all*.'

Joe was right—it wasn't mine either. The gravel in front of Katrina's daddy's place had three or four expensive show-off cars and there was a guy cleaning one though it didn't need it and another guy pushing a shiny wheelbarrow across the huge, too-bright-and-plasticky lawns. All it needed was a cocktail party with the Duchess of Somewhere and Sir Doddery Old Fart and 'Oh, how *awfully* refreshing to see you again', and '*Please*, my dear, *do* go first', and 'Didn't the filly just run a *divine* race yesterday?'

Somewhere right in this same moment Silver Wind was shut up, away from the sun, away from the plants she loved. Whoever lived here would probably approve, I thought. *This* . . . well, this wasn't real and never had been.

While I was shut in with my feelings, Joe and Stefan had shaved and washed: thank you, Maidenhead bus station toilets. Now Stefan produced some bits of make-up and a tiny mirror, stuff he'd bought for me in London without saying anything, planning it all in advance, the pig. Apparently Joe and I were going in too. *He* said it was important not to get separated and he didn't know how long he'd be; but I reckon he was just terrified of seeing his ex again, or her family, and wanted us as reinforcements.

So now we were all stood in the bushes at the end of that drive in our charity-shop best, looking like something no cat would ever want to bring in.

'We'll get thrown out,' I said.

'No . . . no, I don't think so, 99.' But Stefan didn't sound too sure. 'Come on then. The important thing is not to *look* embarrassed or as if we shouldn't be here. We'll give the main entrance a miss, I think, and make our way round the back. There's a sort of servants-and-family entrance there into a little hall next to the kitchen . . . ' He strode off out on to the drive and Joe shrugged, took my hand firmly, and led me out after him. Did they keep dogs, I wondered?

Well, the first taste of Number 1's ex, when she was fetched by some servant to come and see us in the little back hall, was just about what I'd imagined. She was pretty and pretty mixed up and nasty and cold. Or so I thought.

'Why, *Steffy* darling! How *peculiar* of you to just appear like this, without phoning or anything. And *what* are you wearing? And where's your pretty car—I didn't see it outside? You *haven't* come to try and claim me back from Adam, I trust? We're very much in love, I'm afraid.'

She'd hardly given Joe and me a glance, but Stefan ploughed on with the social rules and introduced us.

To me she said, like I was five, 'What a *pretty* girl you are, Kez,' and my name sounded like a horrible taste in her mouth. Joe just got a frosty nod. Then she turned back to Stefan and said, 'I can't stay chatting long, I'm afraid. Adam will need me. (*For what?* I wondered.) Perhaps you should explain why you are here with these . . . people, looking, quite frankly, as if you'd been dressed by the local charity shops.'

How had Stefan gone from warm, caring Rose to this? He said quickly, before I could get something out about why charity shops were a better idea than sweat shops, 'I'm afraid we've come to ask for help. We're in quite a lot of trouble as it happens . . . '

And for a tiny moment I saw a bat-squeak of hurt on Katrina's face and wondered whether a little bit of her really *had* hoped that Stefan was there like some knight to claim his lady, to snatch her away from the hands of the mysterious Adam. Funny, but after that, even though she was a monster, I found it hard to really hate her.

Not that she suddenly came over all worried and told us to come in and chill out and make ourselves at home or anything. No chance. Katrina reluctantly gave her cold and royal permission for us to hang about out of the way—outside—and '*try* not to let anybody see you until I've managed to think of something to tell them myself'. It wasn't a promise of help. Just permission to hang about . . . until later, when we could present ourselves, bowing and scraping or whatever, to her parents and to *darling*

Adam. Then the whole stoating lot of them would kindly decide our fate, apparently. Maybe Princess Katrina wasn't allowed to decide big things for herself!

Funny ideas of friendship some people have.

Knackered and fed-up, especially Stefan I reckon, we decided the most out-of-the-way spot was down next to the river, where the family had a little landing stage, quite well screened from the back of the house. We all had 10p paperbacks from The Cancer Foundation to pass the time: a Dick Francis mystery for Stefan, something funny-sad-happy about a rebellious schoolboy called Pennington for me, and a biography of B.B. King for Joe. Apparently he'd always wanted to learn guitar.

Joe, not B.B. King.

I lay down and opened my book, then dived right down in the inner storms again. The relief of knowing *something*, of having some solid contact with the 'enemy', was huge. But burrowing through this relief like black worms came so many doubts and questions that all the good would soon have flown away.

Two questions banged away at the inside of my skull, again and again.

Was *he*—that voice—telling the truth about Mum being OK now? Was he telling the truth about Mum being released?

The temptation to believe that just doing nothing would bring her back safe was overwhelming. Just lying here in the sun, till she came back to me, the boards warm against my tummy through the cotton . . .

I thought of my wish on the bench in choking Camberwell.

'You two'll have to sit looking the other way for a while,' I said, 'I'm gonna swim.'

'Kez!' Stefan looked up from his book to argue but quickly looked away again and hauled Joe round too to face the back of the house. 'What about Katrina? For God's sake keep *something* on at least!'

I was already diving in, deliciously, lost to the sensation.

When I pulled myself out of the water again, I had decided.

Maybe in this part of my story I'm gonna seem—or already seem—like a bossy, unpleasant bitch, too full of myself for a thirteen-year-old. If that's what you think, fine, but please try to understand that even with Rose's kindness and all that it was like I'd been tied up or weighted down with rocks all that time in Camberwell, so that when the chance came to skip that scene I really felt like I was the butterfly coming out of its pupa.

I was *strong*. OK, only some thirteen-year-old girl; some scruffy, not-very-polite crusty girl maybe you think . . . but the fizzing, tingling power of the Goddess was coming right back through me at last as we headed back to freedom, with summer opening everything up and sending the blood wild with joy.

Does what I'm saying touch anything in you? I hope so.

My eyes or my heart seem to see a lot of stuff clearly, but just what you think of me is hidden, and it *matters*. I didn't know how much it would matter, to be honest. I've started to believe that someone really *will* read this (which I never believed at the start)—you, whoever you are, right *now*—and they'll get to see me spread out over all the pages, pegged out like a poor frog on a board that they tried to get me to cut up at my last school.

Being in Maidenhead was probably the strangest bit of the whole journey.

Katrina managed to get Stefan a suit from somewhere for the family inquisition and he was able to slip back easily into his impressive Civil Service self: quiet, 'well-spoken' (whatever *that* means), a responsible adult looking after two slightly wild children who'd got themselves into all sorts of trouble.

Huh! As if.

But even then, to tell *any* sort of version of the story you had to say things that the refined ears of Katrina's family and fiancé found difficult to hear without acting as if you'd walked oily footprints over their thick cream rugs. Thugs, burning cars, drug barons, suspicious genetic projects . . . you could see that they found it all difficult to believe, even coming from the mouth of someone they'd thought one of *them*.

Like so many, they just blindly hung on to some crazy idea that the police couldn't be wrong and the government couldn't be doing anything against the law and so whatever was happening to us, we must have brought it on ourselves by stepping out of line.

Katrina's gruff old dad, with watery eyes and a great red nose, said, 'Seems to me the best thing is for you to go on back and sort it all out. See if you can't get your job back, Stefan my boy. You don't want to throw that all away over some nonsense like this. Whatever these children have done, I'm sure the authorities will be lenient.'

Darling Adam, who turned out to be a wimpy-looking army guy from some training school, was even worse. 'At any rate, it's hardly fair to appear down here and risk compromising *our* good standing, old man. (*People really say that?*) Whatever you might think of your own career, I'm rather attached to mine. I must say that having heard Kat sing your praises quite a lot *despite* the awful way you treated her, well, I'm rather disappointed in what I see.'

You couldn't blame him for being a bit peed off that Stefan had popped up unexpected, I guess, but I certainly *did* blame him and all the others—even Katrina's weak, hand-wringing, unhappy mum with her nervous little giggle and refusal to even *look* at Joe—for the way they all just thought we must have done something terrible to get people after us. None of them had the imagination to think maybe, just maybe, we were in the right.

They should've lived in the days of the Empire: 'Johnny Foreigner can't *help* what he is, perhaps, but at least we can show him how to be the best he can be.' It was the same when people like that met Travellers, the same bullet-proof, naive, sick-making prejudice.

I was pretty stoating close to just getting up and walking out of there and I think Joe felt the same. I would even prove them right by smashing some vase or something as I went. Lovely thought. But amazingly, before raw feeling veered up too high in me as it sometimes does, Katrina herself spoke up for us.

'If they stay out of sight, Daddy, and promise to go by Monday or perhaps Tuesday at the latest (it was Saturday now) . . . well, I know they've behaved a little strangely, but maybe after that time here we will have convinced them to go back. I don't see that it can do *us* any harm, can it, Daddy?'

By convince 'them' she meant Stefan, I thought. She meant bring him back to the straight-and-narrow, get him to dump the runaway trashy kids, show him how good he could have it with her lot. Was a little bit of her also imagining getting Stefan so grateful for his rescue from disaster at her hands that . . .

Or perhaps that was just my imagination?

Whatever, when she said 'Daddy' in that sweet way, the poor old man was beaten, and since *his* word was law for simpering wifey and wanting-to-impress Adam, she got her way and we stayed.

Adam, feeling threatened, made one last attempt.

'Sir! I really must advise most strongly not to risk unpleasantness or scandal by having these people under your roof.'

But the sugary, little-girl 'Daddy' was too much for him.

Right at the top of the house and at the back, under the shadowy roof eaves, there were a couple of little rooms that had once been a nursery for Katrina and her older brothers, plus bed-sitting room for whichever poor person got hired to amuse them . . . and this is where we were put, caught in a bubble out of real time.

All the people in Kat's family told us in their own charming way to stay up there, out the way, unseen, not bringing some *scandal* on their lovely heads. With a gas ring—somebody left a box of bread, tea bags, and out-of-date tinned food outside our door—and a loo and all that, keeping out the way was easy and gave us a chance to talk about what we could do next.

I sat on the cool lino, next to toy soldiers and a rocking horse, and said clearly, 'I'm still going back down there. Even with the phone call.'

Nobody grabbed me and shook me or laughed out loud. Nobody asked *where* I meant.

'Why, exactly?' Stefan asked, after a minute.

I tried to gather thoughts that had been spinning free all day. 'I think . . . I think that I don't trust the man I heard. Instinct maybe. Or what they've done to protect themselves so far. Or you saying that the government could've got mixed up with people they can't properly control . . . I don't know. Maybe none of those.'

'OK, let's say you're right. What would you do once you were there? We'd never get into that farm without help. Even if she *is* there. They must watch it day and night. They could have dogs, who knows what.'

Joe said, 'What about the papers? Those guys *gotta* be interested in this test, huh? If we get people knowing 'bout this, how can they kill your mother?'

It sounded great. We could blow the whole secret for those idiots, make it public and then, as Joe said, how *could* they hurt Silver Wind, with so many people watching?

But still they might. That farmer: those guys at the Elephant: the man on the phone. It just needed one of them to risk murder to avoid a kidnapping charge. Or just one that wanted to hit back at me and Mum.

If we trusted them to be sensible with the papers and TV and everything homing in on them, we might just as well trust them to be sensible about their promise to let Mum go free.

Like I said, I *didn't* trust them.

Which left me with the pea-brain idea of heading back towards Rook Rise and the tainted, rotten wheat, hoping most of all to bump into Troll in some unlikely way; and if not, then just waiting and watching the farm, looking for signs that Mum was really inside, ready to try and do *something* to get her out if the chance came or if the danger to her seemed to be worse.

Yeah, I know.

So what would *you* do, then?

Katrina came up a few times to see us, that weekend, or to see Stefan anyway. I think what she really wanted was for the wild children to be left up out of the way, out of mind, and 'Steffy' to go back down to join the reptiles.

Maybe he was a bit tempted too, hearing what I wanted to do. She was certainly laying it on pretty thick, only needed a sign saying 'have me' round her neck. I *knew* Joe was with me: but for a while I thought it'd just be the two of us, that once-gypsy Stefan was too used now to comfort and rich people and all the crap that went with his Civil Service lifestyle. Anyway, he'd done enough, hadn't he? No way could I ask more, if he decided to head for Kat's arms and guaranteed hot food, razors, TVs . . .

I worried too about Kat turning us in while we were there, phoning somebody even if Stefan got into trouble. Let's face it, none of them had any idea how *much* trouble we were in, couldn't even imagine it.

'What if she decides to punish you by bringing the enemy here?' I asked Stefan on the Saturday night.

'Punish me for *what* exactly?' he said.

I don't know whether to feel sympathy or disgust for male helplessness at times.

By Sunday evening I'd finished the story about the boy Pennington and spent about half an hour crying afterwards, not because the ending was sad (it wasn't!), but more because the book seemed really *true* to me and true things fill me with . . . something, I don't know what.

They touch my spirit.

My mum, Silver Wind, is the truest thing I know. I ached for her and kept my face to the open window so the others wouldn't see my tears. Outside for the first time in so many weeks there was a haze in the air, a bit of a darkening in the clear blue evening, and my skin was sticky, longing for another plunge into the water.

'A storm?'

I hadn't even heard Joe come up behind me, hadn't known his thoughts had run with mine. His hands met over my belly and I allowed myself for once to lean back on his strength.

'Yes,' I murmured, 'a storm. We need it. But I'm so frightened.'

The last part was just a breath, impossible for him to hear maybe. And then I was crying again, really sobbing like a little girl, and Joe didn't say anything but just held me in his arms, and his skin was cool, untouched by the coming storm.

The storm hadn't come yet the next morning, or not that one anyway. The one that *did* break was a spiteful, little-boy one.

I wake early usually. The light always finds me. I wasn't awake, though, when Kat burst in to the nursery that Monday.

'Quick!' she hissed urgently; then louder, 'Quick! Go! Come *on*, get up and *go*! Adam's phoning *now*. Right now! We had a row about it last night . . . Come *on*!'

We were all three awake now, surfacing in our borrowed blankets, and Stefan managed a bleary:

'What? What's happening, Kat?'

She looked like she could easily have screamed at him, but instead she very patiently and slowly said:

'Adam — is — phoning — the — police — right — now — to — tell — them — about — *you*!'

By the time she reached the last word, almost shrieking it as her patience gave way, we were half packed and pulling on clothes as we thrashed towards the door.

'Here!' Katrina said. 'Take it! It's all I've got in the house.' And she bunged a fifty pound note at Stefan, before pushing him towards the door.

The wild, scandalous, runaway children were right behind, one of them at least thinking that Kat was really OK after all. Better than OK.

No use her hearing it from *me* though.

Jogging away down the lanes away from danger and towards the sheltering crowds of Maidenhead, I gasped to Stefan, 'You came too.'

He shook his head slightly as he ran.

'You really are a clot, 99.'

It came to me then that somewhere under all the steaming upper-class manure poor Kat had inherited, she was the most human of them all and what she really liked about Stefan was that he *was* loyal and decent.

14

If Troll's original timetable for the altered wheat crop was right, we had seven days or perhaps a bit more until the harvest.

After Adam's tip-off would the thugs have guessed where we were heading? Would they know we didn't trust their offer? They'd certainly be policing all the area round Rook Rise Farm like crazy and probably searching in Basingstoke too. The whole thing was a disaster: they could even decide to move Silver Wind somewhere else and we wouldn't know where, although Stefan reckoned, like Troll before, that they'd still feel happier just using one site.

(Who was I to argue with an expert on pedestrian crossings!)

Then there was the weather. When it finally turned and the gathering heaviness became rain, sleeping rough would get pretty nasty. I could make a bender, sure, but then people would spot us a lot more easily. Oh, a bender is like a sort of home-made tent that you can make with material over bendy bits of wood or plastic.

The one *good* thing was money. However it turned out, our stash of earnings plus Kat's fifty could keep us fed and everything at least for the week or more. No need to busk or wash up or anything where we'd be in public. The money helped us get away from Kat's too. We got a bus that was heading north-west for Oxford—they'd never be checking out anything going *that* way—then got out a little way up at some place called Wallingford, walked west a bit to Didcot, then another bus right down to Winchester, even further south than Basingstoke.

The getaway route was Stefan's. Having worn a suit again and brushed with his rich 'friends' he was more like when I first met him, much more in control, thinking very clearly.

'All right,' he said, 'I know it's going to take quite a chunk of the money, but if we follow this route we'll actually end up coming into Basingstoke from the *south*, which I really don't think they'll expect.'

Joe had never been outside London until he met us and I was deep into thoughts of Mum and possibilities for rescue, so for the moment we let Number 1 guide us. The travel took two days, two more days to come up with brilliant ideas, which of course we didn't. We just ended up getting snappy with each other as each thing suggested got crazier and crazier.

'It's gotta be the papers or the TV. There ain't no other way, girl.'

Joe's comment, about the sixth time we'd got to this point, was made on the last bus, the one from Winchester up to Basingstoke. Already we could see the smudge of our destination up ahead.

For the sixth time I bitchily told him why ringing up the newspapers might not be the greatest plan in the world. 'Joe, *dear* Joe . . . can't you stoating see that the press aren't really going to help get Mum back. More likely get her killed, even if they *do* believe us and come stomping down all round Rook Rise Farm. For the Goddess's sake *try* to remember that getting Mum out is the main thing. Imagine it was your mum, OK?'

Help! That was so stupid. Even as I said it I remembered what his mum was, what his life in London was. What was wrong with me?!

Joe got a bit grim and closed off for a while, just looked out at the scenery, and I left him in his silence and felt a monster.

Stefan signalled to me to change places with him and the two of them chatted quietly until we got to Basingstoke, without me being able to hear about what. For the third time in two months I was back in this place, saw buildings that I recognized go past, even the police station. I could imagine *that* building totally flattened. Even better, me flattening it myself with one of those huge crane things that have a swinging iron ball, no warnings given to those inside. I recognized the mood in me; just like with the axe before, a wildness that I could hardly control, building up for days now. I wondered if I was maybe a psychopath or something and prayed to the great Mother Spirit to bring some balance to her wild child.

Maybe the prayer worked too, because as the bus pulled creakily into its bay and we stepped down onto the concrete of the station I found I was laughing quietly, the tension slipping away. Joe was still prickly and not looking at me—who could blame him!—so I grabbed his hand, said 'Wait there a sec,' to Stefan, and hauled him round the nearest corner, out of sight.

'What you at, girl?' He irritably tried to brush me away.

I didn't answer, just lifted his hands, one at a time, to my lips. Then mouthed, 'I'm sorry!' with a pantomime sad-crying face, so that after a struggle not to he had to crack a smile.

I buried my face in his jacket.

When we came back all cuddly and friends again, Stefan, who was alone now on the bay, said sarcastically, 'Well, now *that's* all cleared up . . . shall we choose our hotel?'

We chose Hotel Rape. Minus three thousand stars. No hot and cold running anything, except for the rats, who could run extremely fast.

A field of rape, that is. Thick and bushy and near as we could get to Rook Rise where we still felt safe and hidden. Also, scratchy, uncomfortable, and a horrible colour.

Our 'camp', chosen by the expert (me!), was hard up against a dense hedgerow, screening us from the lane but meaning we'd hear if something or someone was coming. But—and this was the thing—people *don't* usually go near rape as it has a habit of making your eyes and nose run or sting like crazy. (Yeah, OK: rats, noses, and eyes then: three running things.) Part of the mustard family, in case you didn't know. Smug face. And if we really *had* to we could probably also worm our way through that hedge too, even if we didn't take much skin with us.

Stefan and Joe complained that they didn't think much of it, that I wasn't much of a Traveller if that's the best I could do, but then their untrained eyes probably just couldn't pick out the right things! *Apart* from the mustard effect, there were 1) no buildings of any sort for half a mile all around; 2) land that fell away quickly so that we would be hidden from anyone who did come looking until they nearly walked on us; 3) a bushy and tall crop (bright enough for the eye not to notice patches of other bright colour; and 4) a bus stop for Basingstoke, a phone box, and a shop all at the end of the lane, about fifteen minutes' walk away because the route was round several fields before you got to the proper gate . . .

Perfect.

Kitted out like aliens with throwaway DIY dust-masks and goggles, Optrex eye-bath, and anti-histamines from a chemist, we made this our temporary base. The cracked and dusty red earth at the field's edge was our table for spreading out (always cold) food, and for playing dice and cards. It was also bed; tickly, scratchy, uncomfortable, swarming with small bits of life . . . and open to the stars when they showed through the gathering hazy weather. No blankets, of course.

Let's face it, I was home!

We all started to get pretty dirty too—the others more than me because they didn't know how to keep clean without posh toilets and baths. Stefan was soon looking like Robinson Crusoe, reddened by dust and baked by the sun, and Joe became obsessed with all the things that could crawl on your skin, so that playing liar dice or anything with him was an interrupted nightmare as he hopped up and swatted imaginary tickles on his legs or brushed feverishly through his hair, saying, 'Can you see it? Did I get it yet? *Damn*, this countryside stinks.'

The poor love was also the worst rape sufferer—'Don't cry, Joe'—but I'm sure he was starting to get into it really. They both were.

It wasn't all games, though, or sitting round. Most of the time was spent preparing.

'Look,' Stefan said, indistinct behind his mask. 'I don't think we can rely on your friend Troll or anyone else. It's just us, whatever has to be done, so let's get ready on as many fronts as we can. The first thing is that we need to watch the farm as much as possible, in case they go early with their harvest, or try to take your mum out, Kez (*If she's there, I thought*.) or do anything else we should know about. So that's going to be my job, at least to start with.'

We both started to protest, but he shook his head and waved us quiet.

'No, it's no good. You two are needed elsewhere, to do things that I can't do as well as you will be able to.'

Hmmm, did he reckon I didn't know when I was being fobbed off from the more dangerous stuff?

'While I watch the farm, I'll also try to get a few samples of the crop, which we'll use later . . . if we decide to contact the press at any stage.'

Joe gave me a smug, nodding look with half-closed eyes, and I stuck my tongue out at him. Stefan ignored our needling.

'Now, Joe, I know it probably isn't very PC for me even to ask this, but I wonder if you might possibly know how to get into a vehicle without any keys . . . quietly, I mean.'

Another stoating thing that I could do perfectly well myself, thank you. If he had me down for making the sandwiches I'd tell him what he could do with his plans.

Joe agreed, though, that he might know how to do that . . . and why?

'Why is because I want you to try and find the pound where the local police hold vehicles they've towed away, and to see if Kez's bus is there and how easy it might be to get into it.'

'We're gonna steal back the Bedford?' I blurted. Wow, *that* was more like it!

'No!' Stefan was laughing at me. 'Use your brains; that would be complete suicide for us. Wouldn't it? Think! We're just going to try and get things like your mum's and your paperwork, any birth certificates and other papers to add to our pile of evidence. *If* it can be done carefully, without anyone being the wiser, that is.'

Oh, Goddess. Boring but spot on, I supposed. 'So what about me, then? Where will my special talents get used in your master plan, O great one?'

'Well, 99, I'd say that you are now probably the least recognizable of the three of us, always assuming that the enemy haven't caught up with your hair situation . . . so you are the most suited to getting what we need in town. Procurement. Which today will be an old bicycle if you can find one, to make getting about easier. And also a throwaway camera.'

Deep, deep breaths, Kez, from behind your mask.

If Stefan and (grinning) Joe thought I was going to stick to shopping, they were going to get a big surprise!

All I had to do was think of it.

Stefan's plan was to try and get things set up so that at the moment of harvest—which could be any time now—a whole load of things would start at once and give us the best chance of success.

First, there was any evidence.

Samples of wheat, any useful photos we managed to take, paperwork on Mum and me . . . all of it would be sent to some Chelsea solicitor where it turned out that he'd already left a taped record of what had happened in London and before. (Even now he was still writing everything down each day like a diary, the clever sod.) Then if things went wrong we'd have something to bargain with, he said.

At the same time, he wanted to set up some way of getting a tip-off to lots of papers and TV people at once . . . but only at the last minute when we knew for sure that the rotten GM crop was about to be harvested. That was going to be hard, but he reckoned that with preparation the solicitor guy could do that too, with just one call from us to tell him when to go with it.

It still seemed nuts to *me*, like I'd said to Joe on the bus before. I mean, those media idiots all rushing down to Rook Rise Farm at once . . . wasn't that sure to be the end for Silver Wind?

'You're right, of course,' Stefan said breezily, eyes sparkling behind goggles that now seemed to be welded on by grime and dust. 'But imagine, just imagine if we can arrange for my contact to release enough evidence to them to arouse very considerable interest—enough to be certain of the necessary last-minute dash down here—and then make sure that they don't know *exact* locations or details until we allow them to. *That* way we'd have another lever, another bargaining chip if things go pear-shaped. During any rescue attempt one of us will stay in Basingstoke, somewhere public with a phone, like a pub or café, and meet the press. And if that person hasn't received a call from us by a certain time to say that we and . . . er . . . Silver Wind (he'd never been happy using her name) are safe and away, then our media friends will be pointed very quickly—and with cameras rolling and flash-bulbs popping—towards the farm.'

Stoating smart as always . . . just as long as he didn't have *me* down as the person left out of the rescue, that's all.

As for the possible rescue itself, that still seemed the weakest point. Basically it boiled down to two of us— whichever two weren't meeting the press—waiting till the harvest was in full swing and then trying to get to the farm buildings unseen, hoping that all the muscle was busy with the wheat. Then we could simply find Silver Wind, free her, get away again unseen, and presumably walk away into the sunset at a steady four miles an hour, hopping off the road if any cars came by, in case they were after us.

It was good that Stefan had worked out things to bargain with. We'd need them with such a rotten plan.

'All right!' he said irritably, when we'd gone round this the tenth time picking holes in it, 'What do *you* two suggest then?' . . . but pathetically we just had to shake our heads. We'd talked about hiring local muscle with our poxy funds or trying to rig up elegant decoy situations that'd have all those thugs rushing elsewhere in droves. Just about every other nutty scheme you could think of, too: but it still came down to an enemy who was ruthless, efficient, and had links everywhere. They weren't going to be rushed into anything or fooled by some mad trick thought up by the three of *us*.

Were they?

I got an old bike OK from a second-hand junk shop on the edge of town. One speed—stoating slow—and squeaky (as I found out when I had to cycle the thing back to Hotel Rape). Ditto the camera, a throwaway job for a tenner.

And then going in again for other stuff the next day I found out what the big surprise was going to be, that I'd promised Stefan and Joe for sending me shopping. Well, I didn't actually *think* of it. I bumped into it!

WPC Barbara . . . coming out of Boots.

I can't help it if I'm lucky. (You just have to believe, babe, magnetize those things you need . . . Smile.)

She was tanned like a nut and in a summer print dress instead of uniform and didn't recognize me until I stood in her way and said, 'Hi, Barbara.'

'*Kez?*' She boggled a bit and then looked really shifty and started to turn away. 'Kez . . . I can't talk to you. Really. I'll be lynched.'

But she *did* talk to me, bought me a cup of tea in the dingiest, darkest little-old-lady tea rooms ever, and listened to my story. Police or not, I never had a moment's doubt about trusting her, or that she'd help.

I told Joe about it, partly at least, when we were alone, and he nearly blew a fuse at the risk I'd taken. As for Stefan, he could sweat it out for now for sending me shopping.

I could make plans too.

15

OK. So this particular Alice had reached the bottom of her drop. The end of the line, the moment of truth, or whatever it's called.

Whether the soft leaves were going to be there or whether it was going to be broken bones, blood, and disaster . . . who could say?

For two months this thing had been snowballing onwards, not giving me time to think, to see the changes happening in me. Perhaps I've only really seen those changes sat here writing it all down for you. I suppose that anything big, any great whirlwind that comes and blows your life to bits makes you sort of re-decide who you want to be and what's important to you.

Even if you decide to be just like before.

That's what happened to me. The thought of being back with Silver Wind, with Troll and the others, exploring, touching what it was like to be alive, leaving no mark on the landscape but making every breath count, diving deep into the joys of the Goddess and not fighting her . . . that was what I wanted. I'd seen other stuff now and it wouldn't suit me.

Waiting the last couple of days before the early Rook Rise harvest, though, in complete sticky, irritable stillness, wondering if we were really going to trigger our rescue plan or not, it was easy to imagine that the cushion of leaves wouldn't be there. I was suddenly full of doubts in my judgement. I replayed the phone call at Heathrow again and again, waking and sleeping, searching every syllable to find if I could after all trust the hidden voice.

There was no certainty, only dangerous instinct. Also the little bit of logic whispering to me that if Mum was still alive she'd stay that way as a safeguard, while there was still evidence against the wheat people: so that *if* the instinct not to trust was right, her danger would come when the GM wheat had been gathered and sent to whatever secret silos waited for it.

It seemed the world wasn't even breathing, waiting for some terrible thing. The sun was hidden first by the darkening haze and then more completely by great iron-grey clouds, boiling and spiralling across the skies. There was a living presence hanging over us, waiting to see what we would do, threatening destruction, so that even the insects and the rats in our scratchy bed of rape stayed quiet.

We had no real guarantee of how long there'd be to wait—only Troll's original estimate—and any plans had been made. There might even end up being another whole week to hang about out of sight getting grubbier and more wound up in the windless heat. Or more. By now we were taking it in turns to cycle the ancient bike three or four miles over near to Rook Rise, where whoever it was would lie hidden in the long grass opposite the farm drive and watch who came and went, just in case they decided to try and get Silver Wind out after all . . . or in case Troll put in an appearance.

We saw nothing.

Stefan had got a selection of samples from the fringes of several fields and some photos and sent them off to the solicitor, along with the instructions for setting off the press-cavalry charge. We'd also got some old tools together for breaking in at Rook Rise. Getting stuff back from the police pound was another thing completely. Oh yeah, the bus was there OK—I went to see it myself and gaze longingly through the high fences when Joe had reported back. Apart from thick dust it looked just fine. *But* the only way in or out was literally under the nose of some git at the gate in a little hut. Joe had grinned and suggested buying wire-cutters, but for the moment we ended up leaving any attempt in that direction, saving our luck for the main event maybe.

So we waited and watched and the air got like lead.

I didn't know which was worse, kicking the dirt around back in camp or lying for cramped hours on end watching and waiting and not even knowing if we were right that Mum was really in there at all. Even if she *was* there they could easily get her out under some sacks or something in the back of the Land Rover . . . especially if she was dead.

That thought kept coming back. I couldn't squeeze it out of my head.

'Let's pack in the watching,' I said one day in frustration, but Joe said, *'Damn*, it's the only thing we got to do right now. We made a plan and now we got to stick with it.'

So we stuck with it. We reckoned the harvest might be on Tuesday or Wednesday next week. Five or six days. Saturday was due to be a full moon, though nobody'd get to see it in the solid, heavy skies that were over us. It was also my fourteenth birthday.

We'd argued for some time about whether we'd bother celebrating. I said no, it was stoating mad to think we could have a good time with all that was hanging over us, and anyway if we were going to keep to the watching schedule we might as well keep to it, like Joe had said. *They* said I was a grumpy old cow and should start making a bit of an effort to cheer up or fourteen might be a bad year for me.

The grumpy cow lost.

We worked out a compromise, which was that Joe would do the whole day's watching and when he got back, Stefan would do the evening while Joe and I bussed into town to watch a film or something. Kind of Stefan, but you already know he's a sweetie, don't you?

Well, that was the *plan* . . .

About the middle of the day Stefan and I were sat playing cards in the baking red dust when we heard something. Not the regular squeak of our old bike being pushed down the lane, but footsteps pounding on the hard earth and the rattle of stalks being ripped aside. The two of us were already pulling on shoes and up, ready to get out of there, away from whoever it was. A moment later, Joe burst through the crop into our tiny flattened clearing and fell, gasping like a fish, onto our game. He was running in sweat and his face was screwed up with pain—from his leg, I guessed, and from the invisible rape dust.

I just said 'Joe!' stupidly, reaching automatically for a mask for him. Being fourteen wasn't making my brain any quicker.

Stefan was a bit more switched on. 'Water. Get the water bottle!'

We helped Joe to sit up, and he leant back against me while Stefan poured him a mug of water. When he'd drunk that he took the bottle in a shaking hand and tipped the rest over his head in a great shower, pretty much drenching me too.

'*Damn* . . . ' he gasped, 'this messed-up *leg* of mine!'

Somewhere in with the gasps and the pain and the rape there were also tears of frustration. Another twinge hit him and he just plain screamed with it: defiance, anger, hurt. The scream went right across the silent, heavy fields.

I cradled him close and murmured, 'Joe . . . babe . . . it's OK', which again was pretty stupid because it wasn't OK at all.

He was better after that scream, though, and told us through his deep breaths what he had to tell us: '*Listen* . . . machines! A line of 'em. Ten, I think. Those big mothers that cut the stuff . . . the wheat. Ten of those machines all headed right on up into that farm, gleaming away an' new. And that *nothin'* bike got a flat . . . had to run. Oh God . . . to run!'

'Ten machines to cut the wheat, Joe?' Stefan was concentrated and calm. 'Ten combine harvesters going into Rook Rise Farm? Is that what you saw?'

'Hell . . . *yes*!'

'How long ago? How long did it take you to get here?'

'*I* don't know, man. Half an hour? *Too* long!'

Poor Joe, who'd once had the wind in his legs, killing himself to get back and tell us.

Stefan was up now, walking around, talking to himself.

'Ten combines. More than they need for that lot. Unless they want to do it all really quickly, perhaps . . . or at night, with the spotlights? That might be slower. Maybe they're trying to beat the rain, if they've heard a forecast. The combines *could* just be here ready for next week, but . . . *No!* We can't risk it. If we're going with the rescue, we'll have to go at once, tonight.'

And that was the end of the birthday celebrations . . .

The nearest phone box was half a mile from us, which I did in a great burst of all my feelings and fears from that miserable week coming out. The hand that took the phone was shaking, and a voice in my head was saying *It's no good, Kez, the plan is too childish, too weak. Even if your mum's there she's going to die, Kez. They're going to harvest that wheat and then they'll kill her for what she knows. You too if you show your face, idiot!* . . . but I saw the hand dial the number and heard my real voice say, 'Barbara? It's Kez.'

Action! Oh, Goddess, we could act at last, even if it was all hopeless.

She's going to die, Kez, said the voice. *Shut up!* I said right back. *Shut up because we're going to do it! We're going to do something!*

When I'd spoken to Barbara, I made Stefan's call—to his solicitor—and then finally one for a taxi to take Joe into town.

What I had fixed up with Barbara was as crazy as any of it. Looking back now I can't *believe* she even found the guts to try it.

She and Joe were going to steal back our beautiful Bedford bus from the police pound after all.

Partly this was because I thought that it was loony not to have something to drive away in and go back to real life if we did actually manage to get Silver Wind away. Partly it was because there were all those bits of paper hidden in the roof lining of the bus, papers that proved Silver Wind existed and I existed and everything else about us: something to show to the press, the police, whoever, if things did go wrong. And like I said, the Bedford was mine and Mum's anyway.

'Just the papers,' Stefan had said. 'Let's just get the

papers.' And when that seemed too risky he just abandoned that part of the plan. But hey . . . that's my *home*.

Joe knew the plan for the bus, of course, and had agreed (with lots of being buttered up by me) to volunteering as the press-meeting person in Stefan's plan so that he could sort it out. Basically, Barbara was going to distract the gate man at the pound by calling by in uniform with some fake question about a non-existent car they were holding. When Joe took the bus out, she would be first in the hue and cry, immediately using her (switched off) radio to call in with a general alert. For the benefit of the gate man and to give Joe time to park up somewhere out of sight a couple of streets away, she would be straight on the case, a blur of committed police work and then take over the driving when she caught up.

It was the world I'd asked for, I know. But when she heard my story (newly back from a holiday she'd been invited—told—to take without explanation), she promised it to me without a blink. Even the bit about letting Joe drive for a couple of hundred metres. Probably not for me, either, but because she believed in her work so much. Had believed, that is. In her personal code, the police force were not there to protect illegal tests or to victimize Traveller girls. The chances were now that she was set to pack the job in.

When the Bedford had been spirited away successfully, she would even join Joe for the press meeting and add more weight, with her position, to what they would hear from him.

Barbara is a bright jewel. A spirit sister.

I *had* thought I'd tell Stefan all about the new plans as soon as Joe had met his taxi in the lane and been sent off . . . but I didn't, because suddenly now *it* was here at last,

I was *terrified*. Even the thought of Joe driving something as big as a bus for the first time, probably banging it into the kerbs despite my warnings and grinding the gears to death—even that went clean out of my head, and I was just 100 per cent zoomed in on Mum.

Nothing else mattered.

Oh, *Goddess* I was scared.

We had to give the enemy time to get properly moving, of course, so though we set out immediately, we didn't kill ourselves to sprint there or anything. Also, the deadline for phoning Joe to say 'all clear' had been set at 10p.m., still more than six hours away. Plenty.

Every nerve in me was screaming. Stefan was just silent, tight-faced. But when we got to the fringes of Rook Rise, moving carefully but fast through country lanes and across the odd field, we found nothing.

No combines. No massive agricultural engines or great lumbering metal beasts swallowing up the golden heads. Not yet anyway. Just the sea of wheat. Pure, dry gold: so peaceful and innocent-looking that I almost couldn't believe it was really dodgy. No guards, no dogs, nothing moving at all under that yellow-black storm-sky.

What if we were all wrong about this, after all? What if it was something else, not the wheat at all? What if our paranoid guesses had missed the mark?

We'd decided because we already knew it to start our rescue from up the track, where it all began, back at the last site, the last place I'd seen Mum, and now we were just sat waiting. The later and darker we could leave it before setting out, the better. But then at this time of year the dark came late, and the longer we piddled about here the more chance of that scum in the Land Rover or one of his mates spotting us. *If* Rook Rise wasn't really deserted after all, cleared out like the *Mary Celeste*.

To tell you the truth I couldn't think at all any more, just didn't have a clue *what* was best. My brain had turned to cotton wool.

'We have a plan,' Stefan told me calmingly, as we lay at the edge of the old site and watched towards the farm for any sign of movement. 'We will stick to the plan. You don't *need* to think. That's why we made the plan. Remember?'

Sure, I remembered.

Stefan's solicitor, Mr Pinker, would have rung up the newspapers by now, maybe the TV people too, and arranged for them to meet Joe by eight.

By ten the rescue party would have either got Silver Wind out or (more likely!) made a real mess of the whole thing and be lying bleeding somewhere. Either way, Pinker's paper-men and women would be ready to swoop in and record it all, to stop the damage getting any worse if that's the way it'd gone, and to blow the whistle on the wheat scheme.

After all, we were only going in to make sure that the wheat people kept to the deal that they'd suggested.

When Stefan and I had lain unmoving and sweating in the dirt for several hours, without seeing as much as a scrawny crow rising from the still fields, even the in-control Number 1 started to freak out and wonder out loud whether Joe had been imagining the giant machines he'd told us about . . . But there was no 'abort' button for this plan and whatever happened we'd either have to go soon or just bottle out completely and crawl away like insects to leave Mum to her own fate and the fairness of the faceless Heathrow voice.

In my head I could hear the same voice calmly describing torture and death. Nothing was connecting in my brain—like it was filled with painful white light, you know?—and my legs were useless, seeming unattached.

Finally, Stefan's hand closed tight on the little black-wrapped bundle of tools and he said, 'Let's do it, 99. Let's find your mum.'

And just like his words had released some tiny mechanism that'd been holding back massive, crushing forces, a sudden rippling wind moved fiercely across the spiky lines of wheat and a few massive drops of water smacked dully into the dust by my face, like mini explosions. At last the sticky silent stillness of the last few days—some kind of Hell if I'd believed in that—was just changing, just about to tip over into violence. And we were up on our feet, jogging softly forward down the wall-line, rippling and buzzing like that sudden wind with released tension. We took the same way that we'd been before, the day we were there with his Jag, because we knew it went in the right direction . . . and next to us the great wheat sea was starting to move, caught in that urgent, gusting wind.

By the time we were halfway down the first field my too-short prettied-up hair was being blown all over the place and then from two different directions we heard two quite distinct sounds, merging together. From behind us, to the west, there was a first massive growl of thunder; but in front, at the heart of Rook Rise, we could hear a load of heavy diesel engines starting up. The combines.

Stefan hissed back over his shoulder, 'It's all go tonight, isn't it, 99?'

You have to admire the guy's cool. I couldn't have thought of one funny thing to say right then even if I'd sat down and concentrated on it for half an hour.

With the wind and the coming storm and the engine noise—after the silent, strained waiting—*I* just thought that the world was going to end. Can you imagine what that was like, that noise after so much brooding quiet, that ozone tang after stagnancy? We must've been 100 per cent certifiable loony to be doing any of this.

Crash. Louder this time. The thunder was nudging closer. And even though it was only mid-evening on a summer night it was almost dark.

Then the second, longer field, still following the curving line of the low wall. Now we could hear the sound of engines very clearly and see the stabbing arcs of light from the combine spotlights, all dancing together about maybe a quarter of a mile off, where the farm buildings must be. It was a guide, at least, of where we should head for. Well, we weren't just going to follow the farm road right up to the door and say *let us in*, were we?

Two minutes later and it didn't matter. The farm visit for the certifiable loonies was officially over. All the waiting and planning and hope shot clean away to nothing.

We got to the end of the field and vaulted the wall onto the track to go across and back into the cover of more wheat on the other side . . . and stood blinking and dazed like idiot rabbits as a pair of headlights snapped on and held us in their beam.

'How ruddy *nice* to see you again, I'm sure. Right on ruddy *time*. Thoughtful of you. Now I can get on with getting my wheat in before the ruddy *rain* comes.'

Crash!

The next peal of thunder swept away my screamed abuse and then I was *on* the scum, biting, kicking, scratching, wanting him just to shrivel and *die*. When concrete hands and steel arms picked me off him a few seconds later, without effort, he was bleeding from scratches on his cheeks and neck and might even be going to get a black eye from where my head had crunched on to his. Stefan was pinned down on the ground by one of our friends with the impossible shoulders, and I guessed it was another that held me squirming and swearing at the miserable, sour-breathed farmer.

He, the farmer, smacked me round the face, but I just didn't feel it. In my black nothingness I spat at him and carried on trying to kick out, caught firm by the thug behind me.

And then . . .

Then through all the noise, through the wind and thunder and combine engines revving towards us, through the nasty, macho threats of the so-called *man* in front of me, who was saying that the little slut might soon be going to learn some manners . . . through all of that I heard a voice that made my heart just *explode* with joy.

'Kezzie? My baby? My sweet, sweet baby.'

And there she was, in the back of the Land Rover, thin, white and pinched-looking and the gentlest and most wise and perfect of all people there has ever been.

'Mum!'

And I was crying and howling my joy and my pain and need to be with her.

'Go on then,' the farmer said to his grunts, 'shove her in there with the other hippy bitch if that's what she wants. They might as well ruddy *enjoy* their last two or three hours together.'

I didn't care about his threats. I didn't care how long we had. I was with my mum.

I'm crying right now, tears on this paper if you could see it.

The way it's come out I'm writing this bit on my birthday, my fifteenth, exactly a year since Silver Wind came back to me. I think I did it like this on purpose. I don't know.

The next ten minutes or so aren't so clear in my mind, which I guess you'll understand.

There were two Land Rovers this time and I suppose

Stefan must've got stuck in the other one with more of the enemy. Then we were driven off, rattling fast down the track, and it must have been a repeat of when he and I got caught before and got driven back to the Jag, 'cause next time I noticed anything we were right back *again* in our old site, the place it had all begun.

The place where it was going to end for us.

Holding tight to my mum I sort of took in without any surprise that there was a bus there now, *our* bus . . . and that more of the huge, efficient nasties had got Joe and even Barbara together against the side of the Bedford. Now Stefan was being pushed over to join them . . . and then us too. There were no press guys, no cameras . . . just the ring of trees creaking in the wind round us, and down across the fields a spread-out line of lights where the harvest had already begun.

I vaguely heard Barbara playing the police card— laughed at by our captors—Joe saying pathetically that nobody had showed up for his meeting with the press, so they'd come here to find us . . . my mum introducing herself to the boggling Stefan while she kissed my hair and laughed gently at its shortness on her wild daughter.

We were pretty much beaten, all gathered up together hard against the lovely old Bedford, up against the spreading purple flowers. Somehow they'd known about the press, about Pinker, about everything. Not even Stefan was trying to bargain. What was the point? And the enemy had guns, cold black smudges like shadows in their hands. I was still numb—I guess we all were, except maybe Joe who was used to guns and was ready to fight on for his new life away from South London gangs. But the numbness in me changed gradually from the joy of having found Mum to knowing that we would die soon.

One thug had opened up the front of the bus and was messing around with a torch. Sour-breath and his men ringed us in and waited. A bus accident, they said, shouting above the wind. The crazy hippies, who'd stolen their bus back with a disgraced policewoman, wouldn't have maintained the thing properly, wouldn't have MOT'd it. That's why the police had impounded it, of course. For safety. And now the poor hippies would crash and die.

There'd be nothing to do with wheat, they said. Nothing to do with the government or Rook Rise Farm. That dodgily-connected old gas cylinder the poor, ignorant hippies kept to cook on in their old wreck . . . well, with the impact and everything it'd just go *boom* and that'd be it.

So sad.

Time went on, while all this rubbish gradually filtered into my head . . . and I suppose at some moment I started to care about living, to look around once again. The guy fiddling with the bus seemed to be almost done. I started going through in my mind all the things he might have been doing, all the ways he could have set up the bus to look like it was faulty and dangerous.

Would they knock us out first, I wondered? How were they going to do it all? Stood next to me, fingers brushing mine, I could feel that Joe was quiet and coiled up, ready to launch himself into some kind of fight if the chance came. Special Joe. I said to myself: *Wake up, Kez! Snap out of it, you idiot! He's right. You gotta be ready if a chance comes!*

Gradually I went into the breathing routine that helps relax your body and get oxygen to all those muscles before yoga or something.

But there were guns on us. And those guys were the best: strong, cold, ruthless. It'd be crazy to think we had a chance.

I wanted to live.

Somewhere up above us there was a full moon pulling

the world's oceans around, stirring the blood; the Goddess as a huntress and virgin lover and magician . . . but below that the storm was now almost fully on us, wind howling, thunder smashing the air, a million tons of water waiting to cascade down onto the dry, thirsty planet: and now the first really bright tongue of lightning fizzing through the air above us so that the whole miserable bunch of us were lit up bright white . . .

. . . and at the entrance to the site, another figure was picked out too.

Scruffy, a shock of hair, a leather jacket, an almost-beard, and a glinting dangerous grin.

Troll.

The thugs saw him at the same moment. Didn't see a threat. Just another *ruddy* hippy.

'You!' Sour-breath shouted, waving his gun. 'Over here!'

'Oh, I don't think so,' Troll called back. 'I tell you what, mate, I'll come some of the way, half of it, how's that?'

'You crazy ruddy trash. You want to die first? Is that it?' Sour-breath couldn't believe he was being defied. He nodded to one of the muscle-men to go and get the hippy. Both Silver Wind and I gripped each other a little tighter, hoping that Troll really *did* have something up his sleeve.

Crash! Another stab of white light. Troll had done like he said and come halfway. The thug was almost there to get him, but he calmly held up his hand and called:

'Wait! Sure I'll come over there, man, no sweat; but first just check this out. You ought to see it! It's good.'

In his hand he held some kind of little stick. It looked familiar, but I wasn't sure.

The thug had halted, not knowing if he was under threat or not, and Sour-breath screamed angrily: 'What the hell's *that* supposed to be? That your secret ruddy weapon, is it?'

'No, look, man! Really, it's good. A buzz. It's a sparkler, you know, man, a kids' sparkler. Very pretty . . . spacey.'

The farmer was breaking into astonished laughter—the hippy was obviously nuts—and even the stone-faced thugs were grinning at the little moment of light entertainment from the sad git with the jacket.

My rock, Troll, grinned with them, like he was happy everyone was all friends together at last, and he lit the tip of his sparkler and waved it about, almost dancing.

The whole thing was nuts, the most nuts thing ever, and we were all held by it.

The thug took Troll's arm, quite gently, to bring him over as the sparkler died, but Troll said, 'No, wait, man . . . look! Look at your wheat!'

And there, about a hundred metres from us, a great flame shot up in the middle of the dry yellow stalks . . . and then another one, a little further down, and then another and another . . . until in all the fields dipping down towards the farm there was a growing line of fires.

I don't know if you've ever seen them burning stubble in the fields. *That* gets pretty fierce. But torching an uncut crop after weeks of no rain is just about the hottest, quickest fire you'll ever see. *This* one was also being fanned by violent gusts of westerly wind and just *leapt* on down towards the advancing line of combines and the farm buildings beyond.

It was beautiful. Beautifully done.

The guys in the harvesting machines and trucks had no chance of driving their loads clear. They just had to jump out and sprint, leaving the metal monsters to be eaten up by the firewall, each one blowing apart as the flames took it.

Goodbye, GM wheat. Goodbye, Frankenstein-like monster crop, poisoning our bread and the world.

From across the fields the firelighters were singing, offering their work to the Goddess. Silver Wind was singing with them, and then there was my voice too. It was a song of pure silver streams and clear bright air and ripeness and birth. Maybe you think that's daft hippy rubbish or magic or something.

What about our captors, then?

Well, the thugs themselves were good, like I said, and they recognized when they were beaten and knew that it was the time to slip away quietly and efficiently to whatever secret power was controlling them, to make their report and wait for another day.

Surprise surprise, *Sour-breath* was not quite as cool. As the fires spread he was screaming at them to shoot us, shoot the hippy dirt with their childish, destructive hatred of progress. Then when he got no obedience from his men he turned his own gun on us, revenge and madness filling him so that his face was alive with it.

Too late.

One by one the firelighters were coming in from the fields. Still singing, they started to gather at the edge of the site. Some I knew, some not. But each one was another pair of eyes, another witness that would have to die if the farmer was to go ahead with this terrible thing.

Still he held his gun up at us, sweating now, ringed by watchers, lit up by the lightning . . . and then lit up by headlights.

Behind him, up the rough track to the site, came a procession of vehicles. Vans, buses, a familiar ambulance . . . and my mates were all there! All the people from the site before and more too. *My* people!

The new invasion got Sour-breath's gun to waver earthwards, checked him for a second while the madness fought with self-preservation, and in that second Joe exploded towards him—like he must have exploded out of

his running blocks once—struggled with him for a
moment . . . and brought him down.

It was over.

The last bit

I am a happy, free, fifteen-year-old Traveller under open summer skies.

I am sitting on soft grass with my notebook and my friends are sitting round me, content with the shared joy of this moment, content with who and what they are. Joe, Troll, Silver Wind, Jake and Krissy with their kid Isaac, Ron the Pirate and Hannah . . . And now I am about to cut the cord that ties me to this story, I am content too. It would be lovely if you liked me, of course, or saw the things I see, but I don't need it, any more than you need me to approve of what *you* are.

Maybe, though, you'd like to know what happened after that crazy night with the fires, so I'll tell you quickly.

The GM crop was completely destroyed, apart from the heads that we had kept to give to the papers as proof. You probably saw or heard the story last year when it finally got printed. 'Illegal GM trials in Hampshire.'

Doesn't sound like much put that way does it? The thugs that had held us and run the farm—and old Sour-breath himself—were all picked up pretty easily only a few hours after Troll appeared, and while they were being arrested the Goddess was giving us her gift of water, pouring the rain down on us, washing her world clean and putting out the dying fires across the fields.

Wow, there was some dancing that night in the rain.

At some point or other, the police must have got word from their masters to change sides again. They threw a few small fish to the public as a sacrifice—the raid sergeant, Gregg, and Brenda Cotterell both got bounced out of their jobs, and the thugs got done for firearms and all that. Big deal.

Against the odds, Barbara made sergeant and stayed in uniform.

The government themselves, or whoever had controlled everything, wriggled out of the frame completely. Total amazement, I *don't* think! *One* junior minister was added to the list of sacrifices and that was it, we were supposed to think the rest were white as white. I heard this man interviewed on the radio, but could not be sure if his was the voice I heard at Heathrow.

I think it probably wasn't. I think the really guilty ones are still out there.

You decide! Even if they try and do this again, you can stop them. Don't buy their GM muck. It's all in our hands, babe, yours and mine.

Stefan . . . well, Stefan didn't decide to go back to his gypsy roots and join us, worse luck. He's back now at his old job, and he drives a TVR. Posh git. He still keeps an eye on Rose and she's just fine and wondering if she should make it an even hundred.

She must *like* trouble. I love her.

Joe's mum died soon after our escape from London,

her liver giving up the unequal fight, and he felt pretty bad about that . . . and then his brother disappeared too. Maybe he pushed Sweet-Talk too far at last. So Joe's one of us now: my spirit brother, nothing more 'cause there *is* no more than that.

He had one piece of good news, too.

There's just a chance they can fix his leg.

And that really is it, babe! I'm gonna add this page to the stack of others and then . . .

Then there's going to be *such* a party.

Also by Patrick Cave

Last Chance

ISBN 0 19 275241 3

When Dad left and I came home from school and found his letter taped to the fridge I coped beautifully. The letter said he'd gone to St Kitts to live, that it was just something he had to do and sorry and look after the twins.

Julian's dad has run off to St Kitts, leaving him to look after his six-year-old twin sisters, with only a cash card and two Fuzzballs, the latest toy craze, to help him. Julian tries to cope on his own, but finds it hard to fit in his schoolwork and running practice as well, especially when the twins suddenly start behaving oddly. Julian is convinced it is the Fuzzballs that are causing the twins' erratic behaviour and tries to find out why—but no one else seems to have noticed anything. So Julian decides to stake everything on one last chance to prove he is right . . .